SOPHOMORE FAE

Uncle Chip Saves the Fae
Book 5

JAMIE DAVIS

Acknowledgments

This book made possible with the generous assistance of an amazing collection of Kickstarter Backers.

Thank you all. You know who you are!

1

Rose

I leaned over the steering wheel, glaring up through the windshield of my red Firebird. The full moon gleamed in a cloudless sky, bright enough to spotlight my every move. "Damn moon. Perfect night for a heist, isn't it?"

Warren barked out a brief chuckle. "You're worried about getting seen in the moonlight, and yet you drove here in this bright red antique."

"Oh, shut it, Warren. If I wanted your opinion, I'd have asked. I parked a block away for a reason. Your job's simple: kill the power. I'll handle everything else inside."

Warren pulled a soft-sided tool kit from between his knees. "I can kill the power and the alarm system, sure. But we still don't know how many goons are inside. All this over a vague prophecy from some obscure oracle? Are you sure this is worth it?"

I shook my head. "There's no such thing as too much risk when it comes to protecting Sadie. This one's supposed prediction is a little too on point for my taste. I have to know what else she saw in her vision."

"You didn't worry about the vision that seer in Myrtle Beach had a few years back. You told me it took care of itself."

I glared at him. I hated when he brought my own words back to

1

correct me. "That was different. The prophecy fit Astrid as much as it did Sadie. After Patty made the leap first, it was just a matter of standing back and letting everyone assume it was Astrid while we went our way alone. But this is in our own backyard. Baltimore is way too close to us, and people could start asking questions. I have to know exactly what she saw. The oracle is a prisoner inside, so that's where I'm going."

"Suit yourself." Warren popped open his door. "I'll be in position at the transformer in five minutes. When the lights go out, do your thing. I'll meet you back here."

"Go. And be careful."

"You, too." Warren shut the passenger door and slipped into one of the few shadows on this side of the street.

Reaching into the back seat, I pulled out a knotted, weathered club —the shillelagh I'd borrowed from Aunt Allura. A sword was too risky tonight, so the Fae club's magic was perfect. One sharp rap, and any human would be out cold.

According to Warren's research, the mob hideout in South Baltimore only contained mundanes, with no Unusuals. They were a local gang who'd cornered the illegal local sports betting market. With a captured oracle in their custody, I had no doubts how they'd managed that. They could back only sure bets and ignore those not to their advantage.

I hopped out of the car and crossed the street with my club hidden, held straight down alongside my leg. I needed to hurry to get into position before Warren knocked out the power to the building. On the next narrow street, the tall buildings spread longer shadows, and I took advantage of that to cast a simple spell. The shadows wrapped around me as I moved from one hiding place to the next.

Once I reached a vantage point where I could see the side of the warehouse, I stopped and crouched beside a set of metal stairs.

A lone guard stood at the single metal door, his cigar glowing like a signal in the dark. He scanned the street with a little too much attention for my liking. Even once the streetlights were knocked out, the bright moonlight would make the approach too risky.

The dumpster on the opposite side of the street would be a closer hiding place if I could make it there without being spotted. But I didn't have time to wait for the guard to turn and look the opposite way.

I flicked a finger, releasing a thread of mana. Down the street, a rusted trash can toppled with a satisfying clatter.

The guard stiffened, then took a cautious step toward the noise.

I sprinted from the shadows and darted behind the dumpster right before he returned to his former position beside the entrance.

Warren was right on time. Barely thirty seconds later, the overhead streetlights flickered and then went dark. The lights inside the warehouse blinked out too, as did all the lights up and down the street on both sides.

Shit. I didn't want Warren to knock out the entire block. Now local authorities might come to investigate. But I didn't have time to mess with it now. I had a limited amount of time to reach the guard before his human eyes adjusted to the darkness.

I raced from behind the dumpster and charged directly at the guard, who was blinking up at the extinguished streetlight overhead.

He must have heard my boots scuffing on the pavement as I ran at him. He lowered his gaze to me.

"Hey!" he shouted. His hand fumbled at the pistol in the holster beneath his jacket.

I got there before he drew the weapon. I didn't need a gunshot to hurry the authorities along in their response to the broad blackout.

Swinging the club up from my side, I smacked it against the side of his head. A pale green light flared for an instant.

The goon collapsed in a heap on the sidewalk. His soft snoring breaths told me the magic had worked as planned.

I shoved the end of the shillelagh in my belt and dragged him over to lie in the deeper shadows by the building. It was the best I could do to conceal him. Right now, speed was my best ally. I had to get inside and find where they held the oracle. Once I freed her, we could make a run back to the Firebird and question her in another location.

With the guard out of the way, I pulled open the heavy metal door and relied on my Fae dark vision to see in the near total blackness. Down the long hallway ahead of me, a figure walked in my direction with his cellphone flashlight shining.

I picked up speed and ducked low, swinging the club at the back of his knees before he could react. He dropped to the floor flat on his back and let out an oof as the wind was knocked from his lungs.

A quick forehead tap with the shillelagh did the trick. I left him snoring in the middle of the hall.

"Vinnie, is that you?"

The voice came from the open doorway on my right. I flattened myself against the wall and waited.

The guy inside led with a pistol in one hand and his cellphone light in the other.

I smashed the wooden club down on his extended wrist, and he dropped the gun to the floor. Pivoting on one foot, I kicked him in the forehead with the heel of my boot as he reached for the dropped gun.

He slumped to the floor, knocked out the old-fashioned way.

I shrugged. Whatever worked.

I passed several more open doors. The ones on the right went into a large, empty warehouse. The one on the left was a storeroom with janitorial supplies inside. I randomly wondered if there were gangster janitors, or if they hired the regular kind.

At the end of the hallway, a stairway led up. I bounded up the steps two at a time and reached a catwalk around a second-floor office space. It opened with a railing on the right that looked out over the warehouse. A few emergency lamps shed glowing pools of light inside the broad open space below, illuminating a few vehicles parked near a closed overhead garage door and some random crates and boxes.

The left side of the catwalk was a large glassed-in room that looked out over the warehouse floor. I crouched down. There were two figures inside. One was smaller than the other and might have been a woman or a small man. I hoped the smaller one was my oracle. Otherwise, I was going to have to leave one conscious so I could question them.

Still squatting, I waddled below the line of windows toward the door at the far end of the catwalk.

"I'll go and see if the lights are out everywhere," a male voice said. "You stay here, boss."

I couldn't make out the grunted reply, but I clearly wasn't going to find my oracle inside. The two figures were the boss and another gangster. I decided to take out the goon and question the leader for information on how to find the oracle.

The door swung in right before I reached it. A tall man walked out onto the catwalk and almost stumbled over me.

I had little time to react. I punched the club's butt end up into his midsection as hard as I could.

He doubled over and clutched at his belly. I stood and swung the club down at the back of his head. A flash of pale green finished the job. Just one more bad guy to take on, and I'd be able to rescue the oracle and finish this mission.

The dim light of the emergency lamps in the warehouse behind me would outline my body in the doorway, so I didn't enter the room. That would a good way to get myself shot full of holes.

Instead, I dropped to the floor and crawled through the opening.

"Get up, princess. I didn't expect you to crawl your way in here." The woman's voice was gravelly, sharp, and entirely unimpressed. It sounded like she'd smoked a few too many packs of cigarettes in her day.

I craned my neck to look up.

A short woman stood beside a metal desk in the center of the room. She wore a man's suit, tailored to her form. Her hands hung empty at her sides. We were alone, so this was the one the other goon had referred to as "boss."

I stood and brushed the dust off my jeans. A faint aura tinted the edges of the woman's body in the magical spectrum. This was the oracle.

My eyebrows shot up as I realized the boss was the object of my search.

"You didn't know, did you, dearie?"

I shook my head, trying to mask my surprise. The so-called oracle didn't need saving; she was running the show. That made her leverage —and a problem.

"It's okay," the woman replied. "I'm used to being underestimated. I don't advertise that a woman runs our group. I let them assume my big brother is the real boss." She nodded her head at the body outside the doorway. "He'll be all right, yes?"

I lifted the shillelagh. "Its magic will wear off in an hour or so. He'll be fine, but he won't remember much of what happened."

The woman snorted a laugh. "He's not that bright on most days, so it's not a great loss if he's missing a few brain cells. What about the rest of my guys?"

"Two others are the same as him. There's one more who's going to have an old-fashioned concussion from a boot to the head." I shrugged.

"Looks like it's just you and me, then. Let's get down to business." She gestured to a rusty chair by the door and moved to sit in a wheeled clerk's chair beside the metal desk. "I assume you're here about the recent vision I had."

"Yes," I answered. "I really wish you hadn't made it so public. That bit about the half-blood princess of old coming of age soon struck a little too close to home."

The woman cocked her head to one side. "So you came here because I made the pronouncement public? Sorry about that. I don't have control over when visions of that nature strike me. Everyone in the bar overheard me when it hit. So what now? You find out how much I know before you decide what to do next?" She showed her teeth. "I'm not so easy to kill, I assure you."

Her bluntness was refreshing. I was so tired of dancing around the family secret. Part of me longed for it all to be over and for Sadie to come into her own as the Fae queen. At fifteen, she only had a few more years before she ascended to the throne.

"I'd rather not kill anyone. I have to protect what's mine, though. You understand."

"I don't know who you are, aside from your royal aura. You could just leave. I don't know any more than what I said during the vision. I saw the next Fae queen. It's a half-human, half-Fae girl with dark hair. That's it."

"If I don't kill you, how do I know you won't keep digging until you discover everything about her?"

The woman pursed her lips for a second. "You don't. But understand, I'm in the business of sports book, as well as wagers on other pieces of information. I want nothing to do with you or your family. Maybe we can come to an agreement of sorts."

"What kind of agreement?"

"You agree to give me a heads up before the announcement goes public, and I'll hold on to what I know until after the big event. We've still got a few years, right?"

"Yes." My mind whirled through the possibilities and whether I could trust this woman to keep her word. I decided that in her line of work, her word was all she had. If she didn't pay off on bets that were owed on time, she wouldn't stay in business long.

"I'll sweeten the pot with a foretelling I can see that involves you."

"What kind of foretelling?" I asked.

"You and the future Queen are about to encounter a great, round evil from the netherworld."

I blinked at her. "What's that supposed to mean?"

She shrugged. "That's all I can tell you. All I see is you, the girl, and a ball full of evil." She crossed her arms. "Do we have a deal with the other part?"

The new information alarmed me, but I couldn't do anything about it now. "I think that's something I can live with. I'll send you the details a few weeks before the ascension to the throne. I suppose you'll use it to lay some bets of your own on the outcome?"

A broad grin creased the gangster's face. "Of course, dearie. I'm all about parlaying information into money. You do that, and I'll be fine keeping what little I know to myself for the time being."

"Fair enough." It wasn't what I'd thought would happen here tonight. But it was a decent enough outcome. Besides, if I found out later she couldn't be trusted, I could come back and finish the job with lethal force. I'd put Warren on keeping tabs on this gang's actions for the next few years. It would probably mean I'd have to increase what I was paying him, but that would be worth it.

I got up from the chair, nodded once at the woman, and exited the glass room. Three minutes later, I was back at the Firebird.

Warren slipped from the shadows nearby to join me as I reached the car. "Everything good? Where's the oracle?"

"She's not coming. I made a deal with her, though. I'll fill you in on our way back to Westminster. There's some additional work for you in it."

"Good. I'm saving for a new motorcycle."

I rolled my eyes, but inside I knew Warren was worth it. He had that special loyalty you only found once in a while. He'd work for that new bike, and I could put this part of protecting Sadie out of mind for the time being.

We headed back home while I mentally checked over the multitude of threat assessments that always floated through my brain. I was the family arms-mistress. It was my job to keep Sadie alive and well until she attained the throne.

2

Chip

"Sadie, come on. You promised to help cut the oranges for the soccer match tonight. You know it's my turn to bring the team snacks and drinks."

Addy bounced into the room, all nine-year-old energy. "I can help, Uncle Chip! It's fun helping Sadie's soccer team."

I smiled. Addy never missed a chance to hang around Sadie's varsity friends. He didn't know why he enjoyed their company yet—but he'd figure it out soon enough.

Sadie had made the high-school varsity team as a sophomore. It was a great honor for a tenth grader, and a testament to her raw athleticism and ball-handling skills. She took well to being around the mostly older girls on the team. They appreciated her ability and commitment to hard work at practices.

I motioned for Addy to follow me into the kitchen. A large mesh bag of oranges lay on the counter. "Here's a knife. Slice them into quarters and don't cut yourself. That thing is sharp."

Addy laughed. He flipped the kitchen knife in the air and deftly caught it by the handle on the way down. "I know my way around a knife. You and Aunt Rose taught me that much."

"That we did. Just pay attention. I don't want to explain stitches to your aunt when we see her tonight."

Addy pulled out the first orange. "It's exciting. The team is playing under the lights on the main field. We can sit in the stadium bleachers."

"Liberty High's their biggest rival. The coach expects a crowd, so we'll have to out-cheer them." I grabbed another orange and started slicing a pile of my own, trying to keep up with my nephew's unnatural Fae reflexes.

We were halfway finished with the bag of oranges by the time Sadie came into the kitchen. "Sorry, Uncle Chip. I was in the middle of a pre-calc homework problem. I needed to figure it out while it was fresh, you know?"

"It's okay. Grab a plastic zipper bag and gather up the sections. Then get the ice packs for the sports drinks in the cooler."

Sadie did as she was told, scooping up the sliced oranges into a plastic bag. I stood back for a second and watched the two of them work. Mostly, the pair were inseparable. They watched out for each other and usually enjoyed being together. I hoped it never changed. Someday, Addy would become queen Sadie's arms-master and chief champion. I would be out of the job I'd had for the last eleven years, but I didn't care. It would mean I'd fulfilled the vital task my brother and his wife had left for me.

"Hey, where are you guys?" Rose called from the front of the house.

"We're back here," Sadie and Addy answered in unison.

Rose pushed open the kitchen door and came in from the dining room. "Hey, kids. All set for the big game tonight?"

"You bet," Addy said. "We're gonna crush them. Right, Sadie?"

"A hundred percent right," she replied. "I need to go finish packing my bag and change into my uniform."

"Go," I said. "Addy, you put on a sweater. It's going to be chilly tonight. Aunt Rose and I will finish packing up the snacks."

Rose watched the kids leave, then turned to me. "That job I mentioned? It's done."

"The one with the oracle? You got her free?"

"More or less. Turns out she didn't know as much as I feared. We made a deal. She'll keep quiet in exchange for a heads up and an invite to the coronation in three years."

"That's easy, I guess." I stopped for a second before saying, "A coronation, huh? I guess we have to plan a whole reception and party, then?"

Rose grinned. "Don't worry, Chip. Aunt Allura will force us to let her handle the details. We'll protest the appropriate amount and then let her take care of it."

"You think of everything." I pushed the cooler full of fruit slices across the counter. "Finish putting the ice packs in here. I'll make sure the big water cooler and the rest are loaded up in the SUV."

I had just put the other things in the rear of the truck when Rose carried out the cooler full of oranges. She set it down beside the big five-gallon water jug and stepped back while I closed the liftgate.

"You want to ride over with us? The kids would love to have you along."

Rose shook her head. "I'll take my car. I have some late-night errands to run after the game, and it will be easier to leave right from the school."

Sadie came into the garage, followed by Addy in a brightly patterned Christmas sweater. I didn't have the heart to tell him to go into the house and change into something more seasonal for the fall. While he had a lot of things going in his favor, a sense of fashion wasn't one of them.

Sadie caught me staring and leaned in. "I told him to change upstairs, but he insists it'll help him stand out for my friends."

I hid a grin behind one hand and walked around to the driver's side. Rose opened the garage door with the button on the wall and walked out ahead of us to her Firebird parked on the street.

I started the SUV and waited for her to move off the driveway before I pulled out to the road that led into our little corner of the neighborhood. A quick check over my shoulder to make sure the garage door had closed, and we were on our way to the big game.

The parking lot was already half full when we arrived. I was surprised and also proud. The ladies were making a run at the state championship this year. They'd fallen just short of it the previous year, so everyone expected great things from them. Add in the rivalry with Liberty, and the student body and parents in the community had turned out to root them on.

I parked, and Sadie grabbed her backpack as she jumped out. I called out, "Go get some, Sadie."

She responded with a wave over her shoulder without turning around. Rose had parked a few cars down the line from me and walked over to join me and Addy while we unloaded the coolers from the back.

"Where do these go?" Rose asked.

"We'll take them onto the field and stack them near the home team's bench. Then we have to fill up the large insulated jug with ice and water from the concession stand over at the far end of the field."

Rose hefted the five-gallon plastic jug. "I'll do that while you and Addy wrestle with the chests full of goodies."

I chose not to mention how heavy it would be once it was full. Rose was up to hefting a fifty-pound water cooler on her own if she wanted to. She had muscles on muscles hidden in that lithe Fae warrior princess frame.

Addy called for help, distracting me from watching Rose walk away. No matter how things had worked out between us, she still caught my eye at times.

"Come on, buddy. We'll make a couple of trips over and carry each cooler between us."

Addy nodded and helped me haul out the first cooler. I had just closed the liftgate when Clayton Heraty walked past, pushing a wheeled cart.

"Hey, Mr. Proctor. Need a hand with that?"

"Sure." I opened the liftgate again. With the flat cart, we could carry all the ice chests in one go. "What are you doing here? Supporting the ladies in their bid for states?"

"Sort of. The principal asked the cheerleaders to come out and root them on, so Mom's here with Astrid. I just hauled their gear over to the field and was putting this back in the car for Mom."

I hadn't expected to see Patty Peyton here. We'd fallen out ever since our trip to Myrtle Beach a few years back. Her belief that Astrid was in actuality the future Fae queen, coupled with the way she'd talked about Sadie's half-Fae background, had sealed our fate as a couple. We couldn't reveal the truth of Sadie's destiny, so we'd had to put up with her announcing it to everyone in the Unusual community who'd listen.

Even though the mundanes in the school were unaware of the existence of Fae and other Unusuals living alongside them, they'd picked up on something special going on. It had catapulted Patty and Astrid to the top of the high school social food chain. I'd shrugged it off for the most part. But I still didn't look forward to those occasions when our paths crossed. I wondered what Rose's reaction was going to be when she saw that Patty and Astrid were here.

Of all of us, Sadie seemed to have recovered the best from the incidents in Myrtle. Everything from our beach trip—and Astrid's reaction to it all—had removed whatever attachment Sadie had for the other Fae girl. She almost never mentioned Astrid now, except in passing. I wondered if there was animosity there. Come to think of it, maybe I needed to keep an eye on both Rose and Sadie tonight.

"We're loaded up," Addy said. He and Clayton had moved the three coolers onto the cart while I was staring at the playing field.

"Good. Let's roll this over and get the team snacks in place for the game and after party."

"When we're done, can I hang out with Clayton for a while?"

"Sure. Just don't wander away from the game." While their sisters had drifted apart, the two boys had remained friends.

The three of us made quick work of the load, and Addy and Clayton took the cart back to the parking lot to return it to Patty's car. The cheerleaders warmed up in a group not far away, and Patty held court with some of the other cheer moms nearby.

I searched for Rose and spotted her at the same time she noticed Patty. Her eyes narrowed, and her back stiffened while she walked over, lugging the insulated jug full of water.

"I see the cheerios are here." She put the orange jug down on the edge of the wooden bench.

"Careful, Rose. Not here. Don't let Patty get to you."

"That's easy for you to say. I'm counting down to Sadie's coronation, just so I can watch Patty's smug face crumble."

"Hey," I said. "Patty and I had a falling out, too. I don't like the way she's been acting, either. There's nothing we can do about it, and you said it would take some of the pressure off of us. There are plenty in the Unusual community who want to believe she's right about Astrid becoming Queen. They're happy to curry favor, and that helps us keep Sadie safe, right?"

"It does, but the information is there if you look. It's easy to see that the clues suggest other possibilities. We can't let our guard down."

"That's why we have you watching our backs." I smiled. "Come on. Let's find our seats in the stands. The game will start soon, and I want to be where I can see everything. I think Sadie's in for a big game tonight. She's been going in as an early sub for the last few games."

Rose glowered one more time in Patty's direction before she jogged over to catch up with me.

3

Rose

"Go, Sadie!" I leaped to my feet as my niece broke through the defenders, catching the crossing pass with perfect timing.

Beside me, Chip let out a piercing whistle, his fingers to his mouth.

Around us, the crowd cheered while Sadie dribbled the ball around the last defender and approached the Liberty goalie. She feinted left and kicked the ball into the right corner of the goal.

Up in the booth, the boy calling out the game over the PA said, "That's Sadie Proctor with the goal, putting the Tigers up one to nothing."

I turned to Chip, who held up both hands to high-five me. Our hands met, and before I knew it, he'd pulled me into a tight hug. I stiffened at first. Then I thought, what the heck? It was worth it to celebrate our girl's success.

Chip let go of the embrace as quickly as it started. His expression exposed mixed emotions I couldn't read. I hoped he wasn't letting his lascivious mind wander in directions it shouldn't.

I elbowed him in the ribs a little harder than necessary and pointed at Sadie, surrounded by all her teammates on the field. They ran back to midfield to reset for the game's continuation. "All that hard work to make the varsity squad paid off, Chip. You helped her get here."

"You did it, too. She's that agile because of all the weapons and martial arts training you've given her."

I didn't argue with him. He was right.

On the field, the cheerleaders began a rhythmic chant, spelling out T-I-G-E-R while the referee placed the game ball back in the center of the field. The Liberty front line set up to try to even up the score with barely ten minutes left in the game. They began moving the ball down-field, where one of the Liberty players took a long shot on the Tiger's goal.

The goalie intercepted the incoming ball easily and scooped it up. She pointed downfield, directing the offense to set up, then kicked a long shot downfield.

It arced right to where Sadie waited. She jumped up to head the ball into Liberty territory.

A Liberty defender sprang to head the ball in the opposite direction at the same time.

Their skulls collided and bounced apart. A flash of white-hot power surrounded the pair, invisible to most spectators since it was in the magical spectrum.

Both girls collapsed on the grass, unmoving. The crowd's gasp cut short as the referee's whistle shrieked.

Then the ground rumbled—a shockwave radiating out from the field's center.

Screams echoed as the quake rippled through the bleachers, punctuated by a few shouts of alarm.

After a few seconds, the shaking ended.

A hush fell over the crowd.

Chip had already left his seat beside me, moving down the row to the aisle so he could exit the bleachers and go to the field. I followed him, keeping my eyes on our girl. She'd started moving.

Sadie sat up, her hand pressed against her forehead. My sigh of relief only lasted a second. A flash of red around her palm told me she was bleeding.

That was when the bench-clearing brawl started. Players on the field swung at each other wildly, pummeling members of the opposing team. Even the refs and coaches exchanged blows. A deep red aura outlined all of them, indicating a spell or magical cause. Could Sadie somehow be involved? I had to get to her.

I vaulted the waist-high fence that surrounded the field and raced toward Sadie. She and the girl she'd collided with both remained out of the fighting happening around them. I wondered why the other girl wasn't outlined in red like all the other human players were.

Chip had taken the stairs and caught up behind me. I worried that he might succumb to the magical effect, so I glanced back to check on him.

His hand pressed against his chest where his Guardian shark's-tooth charm hung around his neck. Good. Its magic protected him from whatever was happening.

I reached Sadie and knelt next to her. "Are you okay? Move your hand so I can see."

She lifted her hand away from her forehead. The collision with the other player had caused an inch-long split in the skin above her left eyebrow. Blood oozed down the side of her face as soon as it was uncovered.

I pressed her hand back over the wound. "Sadie, listen to me. Something is happening. Are you doing this? Reach inside and try to stop it."

"It's not me, Aunt Rose. I swear. I don't know what happened."

Chip gripped my shoulder and pointed. I followed his finger to the soccer ball lying on the ground about ten feet away.

The same red nimbus of power surrounded the ball, which quivered and spun in place on the ground. A deep hum emanated from the surrounding area.

One of the Liberty players ran at us, her fist raised over her head. She skidded to a stop a few feet from us. The red magical aura had disappeared from her, and she stared blankly around, confused and disoriented.

Another player got knocked to the ground beside us, and she, too, lost the nimbus of the spell's effects when she landed.

"Sadie," I said. "You may not be causing it, but you're the solution. The power within you is canceling the magic. Can you extend your personal aura outward? Draw upon your mana and try."

She closed her eyes, squeezing them shut while she tried to concentrate. I watched around us for a sign she was expanding her circle of calm. Parents and other spectators had come down to the field. As soon as they stepped onto the pitch, their eyes glazed over, and the red aura took them, drawing them into the brawl.

Chip said, "The ball is causing the spell. It has to be."

I helped Sadie stand. "Come on, we have to stop this before someone is seriously injured." She wobbled a little, and I pulled her arm over my shoulder and walked her toward the quivering soccer ball. I didn't understand why it was the locus of this powerful magic, but I knew it had to be stopped.

The ball's shaking increased as we neared, its outline blurring. When we stood beside it, the red aura faded from the brawling humans all around me. The ball still radiated evil energy, but Sadie's magical power countered it.

"Pick it up. Hold it close and see if you can stop it entirely."

Sadie swayed as she bent, her hands trembling as they gripped the ball. The moment she touched it, the red glow flared one last time before vanishing.

Sadie straightened, holding the ball in front of her. "What do I do?"

"I don't know," I replied. "Give me a second to figure it out. Just don't let go of that ball."

She staggered, and I steadied her.

Chip stood on her other side. "She needs to get to the hospital. At the very least, she needs some stitches for that cut. I'm worried she might have a concussion, too."

"Agreed." I nodded at the far end of the field and the parking lot beyond. "Let's go. Things will settle out here now that we've contained the ball's magic effect. We'll take it with us."

We passed Addy and Clayton. Their eyes were wide as they stared at the field.

"Is Sadie okay?" Addy asked.

"She is." Chip pointed back at the stands. "You stay with Clayton and go home with Miss Patty. We have to take Sadie to get some stitches, that's all. I'll text you and Miss Patty when I'm coming to pick you up."

Addy nodded and went with Clayton to find his mom. I didn't like that Chip had gotten Patty involved in this, but it couldn't be helped. We'd deal with any fallout from that later.

Chip and I got Sadie loaded up in the SUV. She sat in the front passenger seat with the soccer ball on her lap. I closed the door. "Where are you taking her? I'll follow in my car."

"I think University of Maryland Urgent Care is good enough. She needs a few stitches for that cut, and they can let us know if we need to go to the emergency room."

"Good." I fished the keys out of my coat pocket. "I'll see you there. Have her take the ball in with her. Make an excuse if you have to for the staff. I'm afraid of what could happen if that thing acts up again while we're inside with the doctor."

Chip nodded and got in the SUV. I went to the Firebird, questions swirling around my mind. Had Sadie caused what happened, or prevented it from getting worse? I didn't blame her, but there was a great deal of power locked up inside her, and it continued to grow as she got closer to her coronation day. This had to be the "round evil" the oracle had warned about.

I got caught at a traffic light, so Chip and Sadie got to the urgent care center first. By the time I got to the parking lot, they had gone inside.

I jogged up and went into the urgent care lobby. A nurse was examining Sadie and taking her vital signs in a small room beside the registration desk. Chip stood nearby.

The nurse held out her hand. "Here, honey, give me the ball so I can take your blood pressure."

"She was awarded the game ball," Chip said. "It's very special to her. I'm sure you can work around it."

"Uh, yeah, sure. Just hold it with one hand on your lap while I take this other arm for the blood pressure cuff."

I nodded my approval at Chip's explanation. He smiled and winked. I guess he thought he had all this easily in hand. Given the powerful magic involved, he was in way over his head and didn't even know it.

After the nurse used some gauze and adhesive tape to cover the cut and control the bleeding, she sent us out into the waiting area again. It wasn't very busy. Only a few people were ahead of us. I guided Chip and Sadie over to chairs in the far corner where we could talk in relative privacy.

Keeping my voice low, I said, "Let's try something before we get called back. Sadie, hand me the ball while we watch the others here in the waiting room. Maybe if you're close by, it will dampen any side effects, too. That way, you don't have to hold it."

Sadie handed me the ball. It no longer glowed with any visible power, and when I held it, I noticed nothing odd about it. It felt like a normal soccer ball to me. I switched to my Fae senses and delved into the magical spectrum. There might have been a hint of a crimson glow around the ball, but I couldn't be sure.

"It looks normal now, for the most part. Chip, use your Guardian charm and see if you sense any danger."

He touched the shark's tooth beneath his shirt. "Nope, I don't feel anything unusual at all about it. Certainly nothing like what we both sensed at the soccer game."

"Sadie, hon, what about you? Do you sense anything or feel any connection to it?"

She stared at the ball for a second and shrugged. "There's something there. It's almost like I can hear a sound or a distant voice coming from it. Is that weird?"

"This whole thing is weird, and I've seen my share of strange and arcane things in my day." I handed the ball back to her. No one in the waiting room had attacked each other like they had at the game earlier. Whatever had happened had passed for now. I pulled out my phone and settled back in my chair while we waited for Sadie's turn with the doctor. I'd put in a little time with Google and some paranormal websites to see if I could turn up anything like this happening before. Wackos and conspiracy theorists ran the sites, but they did a fair job of tracking these kinds of things.

We waited a half hour and then went back to get Sadie checked out. The doctor pronounced a mild concussion. He used super glue, of all things, to close up the cut over Sadie's eye and told us to see her pediatrician within the next week about the concussion. He said she was done with soccer until her regular doctor cleared her.

That news deflated Sadie more than everything else that had happened. When we walked out to the parking lot, she said, "I have to finish the season. I don't want people to think I gave up."

"No one is going to think that," Chip said. "Besides, we don't know how long you'll have to sit out. We'll see Dr. V and get her opinion on what to do next. I'll call her office first thing in the morning. You're not going to school tomorrow until we figure out what happened, anyway." He caught my eye, searching for input.

I nodded. "Good idea. I'll do some more research and check in with a few resources. I'll be at the house in the morning for breakfast. How about I pick up Dunkin' frozen lattes for everyone, along with some donuts?"

"I won't say no to that. What do you think, Sadie?"

"I'd like that." She held up the soccer ball. "What about this? Do I have to sleep with this thing?"

I shook my head. "No, just keep it close by for now. We don't need a random riot starting in the neighborhood while you're sleeping. Hopefully, I'll turn up some answers by morning."

Chip stopped at my Firebird. "Why don't you take Sadie home and sit with her there until I get back from picking up Addy? I'll let Patty know I'm on my way to get him. Unless you want to pick him up?"

Given the wry grin on his face, he already knew my answer. Patty would have a million questions, and every one of them would insinuate it was Sadie's fault. If I had to face her tonight, I might throttle her. Better let Chip handle it.

"Get in, Sadie. We'll get you home, and then I'll start my research."

Sadie climbed into the passenger seat, and I waved at Chip as he headed off. I pulled out of the parking lot and started back to our quiet little corner of the world. Answers about the night's events would have to come later.

4

Chip

When I called, Patty said Addy and Clayton were playing video games at her house. Her clipped tone left me uneasy, but I let it go for the moment. I knew the real questions would come when I got there.

I wasn't wrong.

She was waiting on the front porch as I pulled into her suburban driveway.

I got out and waved. "Hey, Patty. Thanks for watching Addy for me."

"What happened? You and Rose certainly hustled Sadie out of there fast enough. She's not dabbling in dark magic again, is she?"

"No. She is not." I needed to nip this in the bud right away. "We're as clueless about what happened as you are. I was hoping you'd have some answers since you stayed behind. Sadie has a concussion from her collision with that other player. I have no idea what caused the rest of everything."

Patty searched my eyes from the top step of her porch as I walked up.

I kept my gaze level and tried to act normal. "What happened after we left?"

"They called the game after the fighting broke up. There were police everywhere soon afterward, and no one had any answers. Luckily, there were only a few serious injuries. The rest only resulted in some bruised egos."

"So what? Do they have to play the game again?"

"Yes, they're going to schedule a rematch. The authorities chalked the fighting up to a freak earthquake and some over-the-top rivalry drama." Patty stepped aside and flashed me her signature come-hither smile. "Come on in. The boys will want to finish their game."

I nodded and followed her inside. "How's Astrid? I saw a few of the cheerleaders caught up in the fight, too."

"She's fine. None of the Unusuals on the team or the cheer squad were affected by what happened. That's how I know this was magic and not just hot tempers. Are you sure Sadie didn't do something? Kids hide things from their guardians all the time, Chip."

"Why do you assume it's Sadie?" I used her own ego against her. "Your Astrid is supposed to be coming into some superpowers eventually. Maybe she's dabbling in things she shouldn't. She was there, too."

Patty's eyes widened, her voice sharp. "How dare you blame Astrid for this!"

"I could say the same to you. There are plenty of others out there in the world who could cause this kind of mischief. Sadie just scored what turned out to be the game-winning goal. Why would she mess all that up?"

"I don't know." Patty paused for a few seconds before she shook her head. "Sorry, Chip. I guess all the excitement has me worrying about things that I shouldn't. Forgive me?" She reached out and caressed my forearm with a fingertip.

I knew where this was headed. "Um, yeah. Rose is expecting me back to take over watching Sadie. With her concussion, I shouldn't leave her alone tonight. You know. Just in case."

That doused the fire in her eyes pretty fast. Mentioning Rose had that effect on her. "Of course. I understand completely. Let me get Addy for you. Wait here."

I nodded and stayed in the entry hall. Astrid walked in from the kitchen as soon as Patty left to go upstairs.

"Mr. Proctor, is Sadie okay? I heard you talking to my mom."

"Yes, thank you for asking. Just a knock to the head. They closed up her slight cut with some special glue and said rest will take care of the concussion."

"That's good."

Patty trotted down the stairs with Addy and Clayton right behind her. Astrid looked like she was going to say something else, but she closed her mouth when her mother shot her a glance.

"Here's Addy. I'm always happy to help. Tell Sadie we're thinking about her."

"I will." I nodded at both Patty and Astrid and led Addy out to the truck.

He climbed up into the front seat. "Did I hear you say they used glue to close up that cut on Sadie's head? That's so cool."

"It kind of was. The doctor said it's pretty much regular super glue, just made specially for medical use."

"Awesome. We should get some to keep around the house."

I laughed. "I think we'll leave the glueing of wounds to the professionals for the time being. I don't want you getting any ideas, kiddo."

Addy smiled and sat back in his seat as we drove home.

Rose was sitting on the sofa in the family room when we got back from Patty's. "You didn't take long. I was waiting for a call that you were detained."

I snorted a chuckle. "It wasn't because she didn't try. I told her other things were more important right now."

That response brought an instant smile to Rose's face.

I let it drop. "Where's Sadie?"

Rose nodded toward the stairs. "She said she had a headache and wanted to lie down. I checked on her a few minutes ago. She's sound asleep. Good thing the doc said that old belief about not letting people go to sleep wasn't true. I would've kept her up all night."

"Me, too. That reminds me. Addy, go up and get ready for bed. It's a school night, and it's already late."

His shoulders slumped, but he trudged off upstairs. He was struggling with trying to be a big kid like his sister even though he was four years younger.

After he left, I asked, "Where's the ball?"

"I put it on the nightstand beside her bed. While she was getting changed, I tried to scry the spell that had been cast on it. It repelled my spell." Rose scowled. "The magic contained inside is more powerful than I expected. I couldn't get a read on it at all."

"Should you call Hitch? This might require someone who's got a better handle on the pure magic of the Unusual world."

She sighed. "I don't want to, but I may not have a choice. We need to get a read on what is going on with that thing before Sadie has to return to school. It's not like she can carry it around with her all day to classes."

"No, that definitely won't work. Her French teacher has said she won't tolerate anything odd in her classroom. She'd tell Sadie to return the ball to her locker. We can't have a riot breaking out at school."

Rose shrugged. "Maybe if we leave it here, the house's wards will contain its power."

I shook my head. "What happens when a delivery guy comes to the door, or Addy invites his mundane friends to come over from the neighborhood? It might not affect those of us who are protected, but it won't cover visitors."

"I guess Hitch is the best solution." She pulled out her phone and scrolled the screen with her thumb. "I haven't talked to him in over a year. He's the kind of guy who likes to disappear when he gets into trouble—and he's always getting into trouble. I'll go home and shake the trees tomorrow. We'll see if he falls out of one."

"I don't know why you don't like the guy. He's come through for the family enough times."

"Don't be fooled, Chip. Hitch is a mercenary in every way. He only came through for the family because I was paying him. When the going gets tough, he demands extra pay before he steps up. You can't rely on him at all."

I didn't argue with her, even though he'd always seemed nice enough on the few occasions I'd interacted with him. Rose knew him best, and I would follow her lead.

I thought back to the night's occurrences, trying to piece together the chain of events that had led up to the ball getting all magicked up. "Rose, do you think Sadie had a flare of wild magic on the field like she did when she was younger?"

"I wondered the same thing. Not that I'm blaming her. It could've escaped her control during the collision on the field. That could be what caused the ball to broadcast violent intent to the weaker minds nearby."

"I don't want her to think this is all her fault. I'm sure at least some players went to get treated in the emergency room after the game was called off. The fighting was pretty intense. I'm sure there'll be a lot of discussion about it."

Rose scrolled through her phone, nodded once, and held it out to me. "And now we've got the social media circus to deal with."

A video loop played, showing the players brawling on the field in a nearly perfect circle around where Sadie and the other girl lay on the field with the ball nearby. I watched the short loop through twice and glanced down at the bottom. It had a hundred thousand views already.

I let out a low whistle. "Jeeze, that blew up fast."

Rose pulled her phone back. She stared at the screen and frowned. "There are other videos posted by people in the stands. This won't go away."

"Hey, look on the bright side." I put on a cheerful grin. "At least Sadie wasn't caught up in the fighting. There's no way anyone at school—or the coaches—will blame her. She was unconscious."

"That's slight consolation, given everything that happened."

"Take the win, Rose. We'll have other problems to deal with soon enough if I know how this is likely to shake out. This kind of thing never ends well. And it all was going along so nicely for the last year or so."

"Don't jinx it." She launched a playful punch at my shoulder. "You're right, though. Let's not borrow trouble. I'll head home and get a fresh start in the morning. Keep Sadie inside tomorrow and away from doom-scrolling her social media feed. I'll round up Hitch and get him to give the soccer ball a look. If he can't decipher the spell being used, he'll know who can."

I walked Rose to the door. She waved once before she climbed into her car and drove away. I pushed the door closed, locked it, and glanced at my watch. It was later than I'd realized, and I still heard Addy moving around upstairs. I needed to get him settled and then get some sleep myself. We'd work through things in the morning with a fresh look.

5

Rose

The next morning, I got up early and checked my phone right away to make sure Chip hadn't messaged me about anything in the night. Sadie had me worried—and not just about the soccer ball thing. Her concussion wasn't something to blow off as minor or not worth acknowledging.

Once I confirmed there were no messages, I turned to breakfast. My stomach growled—a reminder I'd skipped dinner the night before. All I had was toast and peanut butter, but it would hold me over until I found some proper food and a much-needed coffee.

While I waited for the toast to pop up, I sent a message to the last phone number I had for Hitch. The mage changed his number as often as he changed his underwear. Every time he got himself in a bind, he got a new number.

I set the phone down on the counter while I waited for a reply. In the meantime, I spread some peanut butter on the freshly heated toast and took a big bite.

The phone pinged, and I got a *New Number. Who's this?* message on the screen.

I was pretty sure it wasn't Hitch trying to ghost me. He knew better than that. If I wanted him, I'd track him down and make him regret trying to dodge me.

With the phone in one hand and the toast in the other, I sat down at the small kitchen table. I dialed Warren's number. He usually had a line on the mage's whereabouts or knew those who did.

"Hey, Rose. What happened at the soccer game last night? My phone's blowing up with shares of the videos from the brawl."

"I'm not sure. We're still tracking that problem down. I'll let you know if I need you. For now, do you have a current number for Hitch?"

"Hmmm, I'll have to check. Haven't talked to him in months."

I sighed. "Me either. He's not answering the last contact I have for him."

"He was hooked up with one of the younger witches from the local coven. I think her name was Gwen, or Winn, or something like that. He might still be with her. She works as a barista at the café in the shopping center off Center Street."

"The one across from the Mall?"

"Yep," Warren replied. "I'd start there. While you do that, I'll turn over a few rocks. He might be hiding under one of them." He chuckled.

"Isn't he always?" I mentally shifted gears while finishing the toast. "Okay," I said around the last bite. "You do that, and I'll talk to this witch."

Warren hung up, and I got dressed for a day out in the chilly fall weather that had closed in overnight. Ten minutes later, I was in the Firebird driving across town to get some coffee and hopefully find Hitch at the same time.

Not only was Hitch there at the shopping center, he stood outside the café in the middle of a heated argument with a tiny girl with short dark hair. She had tattoos peeking out along her neck and sleeves and stood on her tiptoes, poking Hitch in the chest to punctuate every word she said.

"You. Cheated. On. Me."

"I swear, I didn't." Hitch took a step back and rubbed at his chest.

She stepped forward, leading with her jabbing finger. "No one. Cheats. On me."

She shouted it out for all to hear. A few shoppers stopped to watch as I approached across the parking lot.

The small woman stepped back from Hitch, her hands weaving an intricate pattern in front of her.

My eyes widened when I realized she was about to cast a spell in a very public place. Even though Hitch probably deserved whatever she planned to do, such an open display of real magic would get her kicked out of the coven. Worse, the local Unusual community would likely get involved. It was important to keep the mundanes unaware of all the surrounding magic.

I raced forward and stepped between the pair.

"Hey, hey! Let's not do anything stupid. No one wants to see this kind of display."

"Yeah, Gwinn. Listen to Rose here. You don't want to hurt me. I didn't do anything, I swear."

"Shut up, Hitch!" we both shouted at him.

Gwinn stepped back from me with her hands on her hips. "Who's this, Hitch? Is this the whore you've been cheating on me with?"

"Gods, no." Both Hitch and I said.

Gwinn squared off, her sharp gaze focused on me. "If you're not his other woman, stay out of this. Buzz off before you regret it."

On most days, I'd admire her spunk, but I didn't have time for this. "Don't start something you can't end, dearie. I have a need for Hitch's services, and I don't want you to kill him before he does what I came for."

Hitch tried on sad puppy dog eyes. "Listen to Rose. She's a local Fae noble. If she needs my services, I should probably help her out. I promise. I'll make it all up to you."

Gwinn stood with her hands balled into fists at her side while her head swiveled back and forth between Hitch and me. After a few seconds, she threw her hands in the air. "Fine, take the bastard. I have no further use for him. I swear, Hitch, if I see you anytime soon, I'll finish that spell I started to cast on you. And I promise. You won't like it."

She whirled around and went back into the café. As she did, the cluster of faces pressed up against the glass all pulled back and returned to their seats and places behind the counter.

I cursed. I had planned on getting some coffee and a pastry, but given her reaction to me and Hitch, I decided I'd get my caffeine fix somewhere else.

"Is your car here?" I asked him.

"No, I rode in with Gwinn this morning."

"Fine, you're coming with me. I saved your ass from an angry witch, so I think you owe me one. Any problem with that?"

Hitch glanced back at the café once more. "Nope. That seems fair enough."

We got in the Firebird, and I drove out of the shopping center parking lot. With the mage on board, it was time to find out what was going on with that soccer ball.

Hitch drummed his fingers on the armrest. "So, what do you need me to do? Don't tell me you want me to cast stronger wards on the house with the kids again. I told you the last time. Even I have limits on what I can do with magic."

"The wards are holding fine from last time," I said, merging onto the highway. "How are your divination skills?"

Hitch grimaced. "Not my strong suit. I can handle the basics, but don't expect miracles."

That wasn't the answer I wanted to hear. Still, I had him with me, and it was worth getting him to try his skills on the soccer ball and see what he could figure out. "Hopefully, simple is all I need. We'll find out soon enough." I turned off the highway, taking a road into town.

"Where are we going? To your brother-in-law's place?"

"Nope, first we hit the drive-through at Dunkin'. I still need my coffee fix for the morning. I'd hoped your barista friend back there was going to help me, but you burned that bridge. This is my second choice." I turned into the donut shop's parking lot and pulled up to the drive-through menu board.

Hitch leaned over to check out the options.

I laughed. "What makes you think I'm buying you breakfast?"

He sat up. "I just figured."

"I'll tell you what. You want something, you can pay for the entire order."

Hitch considered for a second and shook his head. "Nah, I'm good."

I smiled and ordered my Frappuccino and a toasted bagel with cream cheese. I added the lattes and donuts I'd promised Chip and Sadie. After picking up the food at the window, I pulled into a parking space to eat.

After nearly a minute of silence, Hitch said, "I didn't cheat on her."

"What?"

"Gwinn. I didn't cheat on her."

"When it comes to you, I don't judge."

He laughed. "That's a lie."

"I guess I should have said I don't care."

Hitch scowled. "That's hurtful."

"What you do with your life and the mistakes you make are yours and yours alone. As long as you're available to cast the spells I need when I call, you can have fifty girlfriends."

"That's what I'm trying to say. I wasn't fooling around on the side with Gwinn. I've been trying to change. I got a job on the side, and I've been saving up to get her something."

"You got a job?" I asked, unable to hide my skepticism. Hitch working a regular gig was as unlikely as snow in July.

"Yes, if you must know. I'm helping curate the county library's collection of magical tomes. They want to know if there's anything dangerous in the mix."

I'd heard about the county's collection, though I'd never seen it. Aunt Allura's many charitable ventures included supporting the library. She'd mentioned the magical tomes stored at the central branch.

I shrugged. "I suppose you're qualified. What happens when you're finished?"

"It's temporary for now. But I've been told that there might be a permanent position in it for me." He held up crossed fingers. "I'm holding out for that."

"Why don't you just tell Gwinn what you're doing?"

"I want to surprise her with my gift. She knows me well enough to understand I wouldn't take a regular job without a good reason."

"What? You're not going to propose, are you?" The local coven frowned on any personal commitments that weren't to their collective.

"It's not so crazy to think about it." He frowned. "Witches marry and start families all the time."

I set the bagel down on the open wrapper on the dash and twisted to stare at Hitch. "She'd have to ask permission, and the local coven would never allow it. They don't have a problem with the occasional dalliance, but the coven is the only permanent relationship they recognize."

"I know what the norm is, but Gwinn and I have talked about this. She wants to go out on her own."

That raised my eyebrows. "Can she do that? I mean, I suppose that could happen. It's just I've never heard of it before. Once you join a coven, it's for life."

"She assures me it's possible."

I sipped at my drink. The hit of the caffeine was setting in, thankfully. "It's your funeral. Just don't get yourself killed before you help me and the kids out."

"What do you need me to cast a divination on?" Hitch asked.

"A soccer ball."

A burst of laughter came from the mage. A quick clearing of his throat followed it. "Sorry, Rose. That has to be the last thing I expected you to say. You suspect some magic effect has come over a soccer ball? How?"

"That's what you're coming along for. I've narrowed down the source of the problem. Now I need you to figure out how to get rid of it."

Hitch leaned back in his seat. "I'll do the best I can. Like I said. Divination isn't my strong suit."

I finished my bagel and backed out of the parking spot. There was nothing else to say until Hitch had time to inspect the ball at Chip's place. Hopefully, the mage was better at this than he let on.

6

Chip

I finally got Addy out the door to catch the bus, and not a moment too soon. We'd been at each other all morning—every little thing he did grated on my nerves, and I wasn't handling it well. I trudged back to the kitchen, hoping a second cup of coffee would take the edge off my anger toward my nephew. Sadie still slept upstairs.

After refilling my mug, I swung around to sit at the kitchen table a little too fast. Hot coffee sloshed over the rim and burned my hand.

"Agh, dammit!" I slammed the mug onto the counter, and more coffee splashed over my hand. Without thinking, I hurled it at the far wall, the ceramic shattering next to the dining room doorway.

"Whoa, Chip," Rose said. She'd dodged back into the dining room just in time to avoid getting hit by anything. "What the hell? Can I come in now, or are you going to throw the whole coffee pot at me?"

The shock of almost hitting Rose drained away some of my fury.

"I'm sorry. It's been a rough morning. Addy and I have been fighting all the way until he left for school."

Rose entered the kitchen, retrieved a tea-towel from the counter, and wiped at the dripping coffee on the wall.

Hitch poked his head in and craned his neck to study the mess.

"It's no wonder you feel that way, Chip. There's a residual rage lurking close by. Can't you sense the negative energy? It's powerful."

My shoulders tensed instantly. I snapped at him. "I thought your wards on the house were supposed to protect us from stuff like that? Are you cheating us?"

Rose stopped dabbing at the spilled coffee. "Hey, easy does it, Chip. Hitch is here to do us a favor. You don't have to jump down his throat."

I slumped into one of the kitchen chairs. "What is wrong with me? I shouldn't be affected by magic. My shark's tooth charm protects me from that stuff."

Rose pulled another mug from the cabinet and filled it from the carafe before handing it to me. "Here, try not to throw this at anyone." She sniffed. "I smell a hint of brimstone and something else in the air. There is definitely rage energy emanating close by. Where are Sadie and ball?"

"Upstairs."

Rose sprinted from the kitchen.

I set my coffee down and followed Hitch, who'd chased after her. We caught up to her outside Sadie's open door.

"Well, there's your problem," Hitch said, pointing at the soccer ball. "That thing's glowing red with rage energy. Seriously, you can't see it?"

I saw nothing.

Rose shook her head. "I can't see it either, but rage power is demonic and originates in the lower planes. Most Fae can't sense it."

"Is that the soccer ball you want me to cast a divination spell on?" Hitch asked. "Because I'm not sure I want to tangle with it. There's a lot of power locked up inside that thing."

Sadie stirred in bed and sat up. "Are you all done creeping outside my room while I sleep? It's super weird, you know."

Rose held out her hand. "Come here. There's something going on with the ball."

Sadie kicked off the covers and slid out of bed, wearing boxer shorts and a tank top.

I pulled on Hitch's arm when I noticed him staring at my teen niece. "Hey, that's enough of that. You come back downstairs with me. They can bring the ball down to you for examination."

"Uh, yeah, sure." He followed me to the steps. "Sorry about that."

"Just so you know, I catch you looking at her like that again, and I won't just punch you in the face. I'll tell Rose about it, too."

"Hey, there's no need to get nasty. I promise it won't happen again."

We returned to the kitchen, and Hitch pointed at the half-full pot of coffee. "Can I have some? Rose wouldn't get me anything at the drive-through."

"Sure, help yourself. There's half and half in the fridge and sugar in that bowl by the coffee maker."

Hitch came over with a mug of coffee and sat down across from me at the round kitchen table. "Rose didn't tell me much of why I was coming here. Just that she had something for me to examine. Where'd that rage ball come from?"

I told him about the soccer game last night and the earthquake.

"I felt the tremors. It never occurred to me to suspect it was magical. It was over so quickly." He sipped at the coffee. "So, Sadie's proximity to the ball seems to dampen the power of the effects?"

"I thought so, but maybe its effects build up over time, or she has to be awake." I shook my head. "I don't know. Hopefully, you can help us figure it out."

The door to the dining room opened, and Rose entered, followed by Sadie carrying the soccer ball.

"How're you feeling this morning, hon?" I asked. I planned on following up with her pediatrician as the urgent care doc had suggested, but I'd get to the emergency room if she was feeling worse.

Sadie shrugged. "My head hurts a bit. I didn't sleep well. I kept having weird dreams."

"What kind of dreams?" Rose asked.

"That's the strange part." She set the ball on the counter and grabbed a box of cereal from the shelf. "It wasn't like anything I'd seen before. I was in a war, but it wasn't with people. There was fire, and rivers of lava everywhere, and the enemies and friends were both some kind of demon folk. They all turned toward me, and I felt trapped, with nowhere to run. Then I woke up." She poured a bowlful of the flakes and added in some of the milk from the carton Rose handed her.

"Demons?" Rose put the milk back in the fridge. "And you've never had this kind of dream before?"

"Nope. Weird, right?" Sadie sat down with a spoon and started in on her breakfast.

I shot Rose a concerned glance. What did all this mean? "I'll get you some juice to go with that."

"That's good. Make me some toast, too. I'm hungry."

I was used to her barely eating anything for breakfast. I jumped into dad-mode and, in less than a minute, had her juice in front of her and two slices of bread in the toaster. "You want butter or peanut butter on the toast?"

"What I want is to smear it with the entrails of my enemies." The voice that came from Sadie's mouth wasn't hers. It was deep and gravelly, like it had crawled out of a hellish pit.

We all froze and stared at her back while she kept eating.

After a few seconds, she turned around and stared back at us. "What?" she asked in her normal voice.

Rose took a step toward her. "Why did you say that just then, honey?"

"What? I just want peanut butter. Uncle Chip asked me, so I answered."

I grabbed the peanut butter from the pantry along with a butter knife and set it down next to her. Then I sat in the seat across from her. She looked like herself. I glanced over at Rose.

Rose pointed at the ball. "Hitch, take that into the other room. Do what you can to find out where its power is coming from. Then tell me how to destroy it."

The mage picked up the soccer ball, tucked it under one arm, and left for the dining room.

As the door swung shut, Sadie whipped around to Rose. "End me, and you end her," the demonic voice rumbled, daring us with its sinister tone.

As soon as she said it, she returned to her breakfast as if nothing had happened.

The toast popped up, and I jumped. I took a breath to steady my nerves and got up. With the toast in hand, I smeared peanut butter on each piece as if our girl wasn't old enough to do it herself.

Rose stepped across to the counter and motioned for me to follow her.

I moved over and leaned in close. "What the hell is that?"

"The ball is talking through her. Isn't it obvious?"

"You know what I mean. How? Her Fae charm should protect her from that kind of thing, right?"

Rose looked back at Sadie, still eating with her back to us. "It should, but something very wrong and powerful is happening here. Remember the earthquake and Sadie's collision? It all happened at the same time. It takes a great deal of mana energy to move even a small piece of the earth, let alone a whole soccer pitch, Chip. More power than anyone else I know."

"More than the wild magic controlled by the future Fae Queen?" I stared at Sadie's back.

"Maybe not. Though it clearly happened by accident. Let's wait for Hitch to get us some answers before we jump to any conclusions."

I was about to answer but stopped when the dining room door opened and Hitch walked in.

He tossed me the ball underhanded and picked up his coffee mug from the counter. He gestured to me. "That there ball is possessed. Were I to guess, I'd say it was a lesser demon from one of the lower planes, though I'm not good enough at divination to be sure."

"Who are you calling a lesser demon, puny mage?"

The voice was back, this time coming from the ball in my hands. I yelped and jumped away, dropping the ball to the floor at the same time.

"Ow! Careful with me. This form is soft and easily injured."

Rose held up a finger to keep me from answering and crouched down beside the ball. "Who am I talking to?"

"Not so quick, girlie. Who the hell are you?"

"I'm the one with the magic sword that's going to end you if you don't start answering questions."

This time, the voice came from Sadie across the room. "Not so fast. The girl and I are linked. You kill me, you'll kill her, too."

"Easy," I said. "No one is killing anyone. There's been some sort of mistake, and all we have to do is find out how to undo it. Everyone calm down. Hitch, you can undo this, right?"

"Disconnect a demon from your niece and a soccer ball at the same time?" He gave a single back-and-forth shake of his head. "Nope, this is way over my pay grade. I specialize in charms and protection spells. Plus, this has the taste of wild magic. I don't know how that got released, but I'm not messing with that. No way. No how."

I wasn't the kind to take no for an answer in a negotiation. "If you can't do this, you definitely know someone who can."

"Maybe, but you need to figure out what happened first. Why was this demon in a position to be captured, and what is it that links him to the ball and Sadie that way?"

Sadie interrupted us. "Hitch, you can't leave me like this. If there's some sort of demon inside of me, I can't go to school or anything. I'm a freak!"

"You're not a freak," Rose and I said in unison.

I gestured for her to take over. This was way out of my depth.

"We will figure this out. I promise." She picked up the ball from the floor and tucked it under one arm. "Hitch, you figure out who you know that can handle this kind of possession. And keep your mouth shut."

Hitch mimed zipping his lips shut and tossing away the key. "I'm not talking about this to anyone, trust me. I'll make some discreet inquiries and get back to you." He nodded a goodbye to Sadie and me.

"Come on." I motioned for Sadie to stand up. "You're finished with breakfast for now. Let's go into the family room and sit down while we figure this out." We followed Hitch into the dining room and then into the family room area. Rose brought up the rear with the cursed ball.

Hitch continued to the front door. "I'll call for a ride on my app." He waved once with phone in hand and left.

I sat down in my easy chair and pointed to the sofa. Sadie and Rose took seats at opposite ends, facing me.

I leaned forward and clapped my hands together. "Good. Let's get down to business and see what we can figure out."

7

Rose

I rolled my eyes at Chip's ever-positive nature. He always believed there was nothing he couldn't talk his way out of. I set the ball down on the sofa midway between Sadie and me, where I could keep an eye on it.

"I'll take the lead, Chip."

"Why?"

"You ever negotiate with a demon?"

He hesitated. "No, but I've outsmarted a few fund managers."

I rolled my eyes. "Not even close."

"How many demonic negotiations have you been on?"

I glared at him. "None. But I've killed more than a few."

"Hey!" the demon bellowed from the ball. "I said what I said. Kill me, kill the girl."

Sadie's eyes welled up with tears. "Can you make him stop?"

I held up a hand, preventing Chip from saying whatever idiotic thing he was about to say. "Let's start over. I'm Princess Rose Elders-dottir. This is my niece, and the other one is her Guardian, Chip Proctor."

"Hmmm, a princess, you say?" the ball said. "High Fae, from the taste of the girl's aura."

"Yes," I said. "Now, how about you? Who or what are you?"

"I'm Gorrath, slayer of millions, marauder of the nine levels of hell, and leader of the greatest army of demon kind ever assembled."

Chip smirked. "You forgot something."

"What's that?"

"That you're a soccer ball."

"What's a soccer ball?" the ball asked.

I couldn't resist a smile. "A children's plaything. You're trapped inside it and connected to my niece. Once, you may have been a big deal, but now you're just a leather sphere a little over a foot in diameter."

"You're joking."

"Dead serious," I said, folding my arms. "What were you doing right before you found yourself here? Anything you can tell us might help us send you back."

"I was leading a battle to complete my ultimate conquest. It would have been my finest moment, but the ground beneath me shook and knocked me from my fiery steed. Then I fell into darkness. I thought some magics from my opponents had trapped me, so I immediately rallied all my allies to come to my aid and battle the enemy."

Chip snapped his fingers. "That must have been when the brawl on the soccer field started. He used his power, and it energized the players on the field into attacking their adversaries."

He was probably correct. "Then your power was stilled for a time, is that right?" At the game, when we brought the ball closer to Sadie and got her away from the field, she must have unconsciously damp-ened the demonic power with her inherent wild magic.

"Yes, that happened. But also, through the darkness, I saw a deep blue light in the distance. I ran toward it, knowing it was my only avenue of escape."

It made sense. Sadie's strange dream and now this description. "When did you realize you could reach out and talk to us? Have you been listening for a long time?"

"I only arrived at the source of the light when you gathered for a communal meal. I could see out through two scrying pools of blue water, set alone amid the blackness."

Sadie looked back at me with her sapphire blue eyes.

"Can you see me now, Gorrath?"

"Yes, Princess," the voice said from Sadie's mouth.

"Well, get out of my niece. Look out through her eyes if you must, but speak only through the ball and only to the three of us. Do you understand?"

"Or what?" Gorrath asked from the ball.

"Or someone who doesn't trust demons trapped inside a soccer ball might just decide you're better off destroyed no matter who else dies. You must have a memory of the demon wars during the human dark ages. People have very creative ways to extract a being from the lower planes during a possession. We could always turn you over to the exorcist cabal and take our chances with the results."

Chip shot me a sharp glance. I glared at him, willing him to stay silent. He needed to let me play this out. I'd talked to a lot of demons before I killed them and learned a lot about what they feared most.

Gorrath hissed. "No, no. Do not involve the ecclesiastics and especially not the warrior priests from the Vatican. I will comply with your wishes as long as you don't seek to double-cross me."

Chip mouthed, "Warrior priests?"

I waved him off. "Then we have a deal. We will endeavor to send you back to whence you came. In exchange, you will communicate only through the ball and do nothing to enact magic or sow discord."

"I swear."

That was too quick.

"Swear it on your true name. Understand that I can have a Vatican priest from the local parish here in under an hour."

"Very well," the ball said after a long pause. "I, Gorrath Miltersop Zendalekor, so swear to abide by this agreement. I will abide while you separate me from this child's plaything."

It was the best I could do. I didn't trust the demon at all, but the oath should keep us safe enough for the time being. I couldn't help but think there was something I was missing.

Chip stood up. "Well, now that's settled, how about Sadie gets some rest? Our guest can stew in his leather prison for a while."

Sadie scowled at him. "I just got up. I don't want to go back up to my room."

"You don't have to, hon," Chip said. "But I want to you take it easy. Don't do anything that might get you—or our new guest—riled up. Got it?"

"Can I play on the game console in the den?"

Chip nodded, and she immediately went to the front room the kids used for gaming and watching shows when their friends were over.

As soon as she left, Chip opened his mouth to speak.

I shook my head and pointed at the soccer ball on the couch. My eyes flicked over to the far corner.

He nodded and moved over to the edge of the dining room table.

I joined him and drew upon my mana to create a minor spell of silence around us to keep Gorrath from hearing us.

"Warrior priests of the Vatican?" Chip asked as soon as I nodded. "Is that even a thing?"

"Ever hear of the Templars? They're the most well-known of the warrior orders. There were others."

"Weren't the Templars hunted down and destroyed by a vengeful French king hundreds of years ago?"

I smiled. "Yes, but we don't have to tell him that. Let him believe in the bogeyman for a while. It'll keep him in line. Trust me in one thing, Chip. Every word out of that ball is a potential lie. Demons are not to be believed or dealt with lightly."

"I've never met one until now, but their reputation precedes them in human lore. I am sure I can figure out a way around his word games. What about Sadie? Is she safe?"

I nodded. "For now, I think so. I have to do some research, but I think he swore on his actual true name. If that's the case, he will uphold the strict letter of the agreement. However, any potential loophole presents an opportunity for him to twist things his way. Remember that."

"Princess, Guardian," Gorrath called from the sofa. "I seek more information about where it is I've found myself."

I cocked an eyebrow up and looked at Chip. "See, he's already angling for a way to subvert his oath. Be careful with anything you tell him."

"I can manage this. Believe me. I won't screw up.'

I doubted him, but I couldn't stay here at the house forever. For now, I needed to check in with Aunt Allura and her extensive collection of historic and arcane tomes. There might be some mention of Gorrath in there from the Demon Wars. He talked like he did, indeed, remember the time when demons and their human armies roamed the steppes of northeastern Europe. If he was referenced, I might find out some more about him.

I dropped the silence spell and stepped back from Chip. "You good managing our guest inside the ball?"

"Sure. It's not like he eats much. I just have to keep him topped off with the bicycle pump from time to time, right?" He grinned at his poor attempt at humor.

"Now is not the time for jokes, Chip Proctor. Remember what I said." I held his gaze until he nodded. "Good. I'm off then. I need to follow up on a few things. If I find anything, I'll text you. Keep an eye on our girl. I'll check in later tonight or tomorrow morning."

I glanced at the soccer ball on the couch. There wasn't anything else I could do here. It was time to find a solution to the problem and do it as fast as I could. I definitely didn't want this creature lurking around threatening my precious Sadie. As soon as I found a way, I was going to extract that demon.

Then I was going to kill him.

8

Chip

After Rose departed, I left the ball on the couch and returned to the kitchen to check on Sadie. She stood by the sink, rinsing out her cereal bowl. I caught her wiping her sleeve across her eyes, a sharp little sob slipping free before she could stop it.

My stomach clenched. I hated seeing her like this, but what could I say that didn't sound hollow?

"Hey, kiddo. Never a dull week here in the Proctor house. Am I right?"

Sadie straightened from her slump and turned to face me. I pretended not to notice her reddened eyes or slight sniffle.

"As long as we find a way to deal with that thing. Where did you put it?"

"Its name is Gorrath. He's a demon, and he's stuck on the couch for the time being. He's promised to play nice and stay out of your head."

"And you trust him? Uncle Chip, he's a demon."

"I know. And, no, I don't trust him. You stay vigilant and tell me if you sense anything lurking in the corners of your mind or trying to get in."

"How will I know? I wasn't aware he was speaking through me until you and Aunt Rose confronted him."

That stopped me. "I honestly don't know. That's a question for your aunt when she returns. For now, tell me about anything that feels odd in your mind." As soon as I said it, I realized that teens weren't all that sure of their emotions or thoughts most of the time.

Sadie must have been thinking the same thing. She cocked her head to one side and put her hands on her hips.

"Okay, okay. Just be vigilant and tell me what you can."

"Do we have to stay home with the demon in the house? I don't feel safe with it nearby like this."

I thought about it. "No, we can go out. It's not like it's going to grow legs and run away. I was planning on a grocery run today. Want to join me at the store? We can get something from the café next door while we're there if you want."

"I'd like that." Her ponytail bobbed as she gave me an enthusiastic nod. "I need to get some distance for a while."

As she waited, I grabbed my coat and keys from the rack by the garage door. I held the door for her while she pulled on her team jacket and grabbed her purse. Sadie was right. It would feel good to get some fresh air and clear our minds.

The parking lot at the grocery store was only half full. I always enjoyed going shopping after the kids left for school. The store's shelves were freshly stocked from the night shift, and it wasn't that crowded. Sadie walked ahead of me and pulled a cart from the storage area by the entrance. She led the way inside while I pulled up the grocery list on my phone.

I pointed left. "Produce first. We need bananas, grapes, and oranges."

Sadie popped off a military style salute and turned past the line of cash registers to head to the far end of the store. I followed behind with a smile. Sadie rarely came with me when I shopped, like she did when she was little. It was a delightful change.

We wound our way through the first few aisles, adding items to our cart from my list.

In the middle of the fifth aisle, Sadie sucked in a sharp gasp. Instantly on guard, I looked around.

Sadie stood by the cart with her hand over her mouth. Her eyes remained locked on the old man approaching from the far end of the aisle.

"What is it? Tell me."

Sadie dropped her hand from her face. "That man isn't a man. He's a demon in disguise."

"You sure?" He didn't look different to me. Sadie, however, had long displayed an affinity for seeing the Unusual creatures hiding inside a human disguise. It could work for demons, too.

I fished out the gold shark's tooth from where it hung against my collarbone. Gripping the charm hard, I tried to attune my vision to the magical spectrum. I wasn't very good at this, and I didn't practice as often as I should, but it was all I had.

A hazy red outline formed around the old, gray-haired man shuffling toward us. He didn't have a cart and carried nothing from the shelves in his hands. The outline around his hunched, aged form was a great deal larger than he was, but I couldn't make out much more than its vaguely humanoid shape.

The old man lifted his gaze from the floor to Sadie and me. His eyes glowed a deep crimson.

"Sadie, get behind me." I reached for the sword hilt with the magically collapsed blade that hung on my belt. I didn't want to kill this guy in case he was only the victim of a temporary possession, but I wouldn't let anything happen to my niece either.

"Uncle Chip, there's another one behind you at the other end."

My head whipped around. A pimply-faced twenty-something boy with stringy dirty-blond hair stood at the far end behind us. A similar hulking red form outlined his body, too.

"Shit, grab something to fight. Anything you can." I cast my eyes around, looking for something for Sadie to use as a weapon. I held up my sword's hilt and concentrated on extending the blade to its full three-foot length.

I faced the old man. He was the closest. "Keep an eye on the kid. I'll take the old guy."

Sadie had grabbed two large cans of soup from the shelf beside her and held one in each hand. I didn't know what she planned on doing with them, but it was that or assault them with boxed pasta or jars of spaghetti sauce.

"Stop right there." I leveled the point of the sword toward the old man's chest.

"Where is the traitor?" the old man rasped, his crimson gaze locking onto us with an intensity that sent a shiver down my spine.

"I'm sorry. Who?"

The man tilted his head back and sniffed. "I sense a trace of him around you both. We intend no harm, but we must have the traitor back."

"I don't have anyone else here. It's just the two of us. Now back away, or I'll use this magical blade to banish you back to hell where you belong."

A wicked grin replaced the blank stare on the old man's face. "So be it, puny human."

He moved fast for his age, but enhanced by a demon or not, he wasn't faster than my honed reflexes with the sword. I lunged forward and thrust hard with the blade at the center of his mass.

The blade penetrated an inch below his breastbone, and the old man grimaced and twisted to the side. The sword's tip cut across the front of his ratty brown sport coat and shirt up to the shoulder. It left a bloody trail in its wake.

I recovered from my lunge in time to bring up a forearm to block a spinning kick. The force of it nearly broke my wrist, but I deflected it to the side.

With a downward slash, I hacked at the juncture between head and shoulder. The enchanted blade cut deep into the base of his neck, releasing a combination of red blood and black ooze. Maybe he wasn't a possessed human after all.

The attack drove the demon backward with his arms flailing. I used the opportunity to check on Sadie.

The demon kid stalked forward—right into a flying can of tomato soup. The impact snapped his head sideways, making him stagger. A second can whipped past, missing, but the third caught him square in the nose.

"How you doing back there?" I asked.

"I can hold him back as long as the cans last." She reloaded with two more from the shelf beside her. Her arm whipped over and down behind her, launching the projectile in classic softball fast-pitch style. "Try some cream of mushroom on for size, asshole."

The fourth can caromed off his shoulder with an audible crack and left his arm hanging limp at his side.

Sadie laughed. "Ooh, that's gotta hurt." She immediately launched a follow-up shot that smacked him in the face again. "Here's some chunky vegetable beef for you!"

The kid's eyes rolled up in his head, and he dropped to the floor, limp like a rag doll.

I wrenched my attention back to the demon attacking me in time to see him hobble away around the corner at the far end of the aisle.

"We need to go, Sadie."

"Yeah," she said, hefting two more cans. "Let's chase him down. He can't get away."

"No, we are leaving." I worried there might be reinforcements coming. "I don't know how they found us, or what the connection is to Gorrath, but we're exposed here, and soup cans aren't an acceptable substitute for your enchanted blade on the rack at home."

Sadie's lip pushed out in the tiniest of pouts. "I wish I had a blade I could carry everywhere like yours, Uncle Chip. Then we wouldn't have to go home for my sword."

"You can take it up with the smith the next time we hit the Renn Faire. For now, listen to me. We have to leave."

She didn't put the cans back, instead setting them on the child seat near the grocery cart's handle.

"Leave the cart. We can go shopping another time." I concentrated and collapsed my blade into the hilt. I didn't return it to the clip on my belt, though.

"Okay, but I'm bringing the cans." She hefted them again, one in each hand.

"Suit yourself. You can leave them by the registers on our way out."

We hurried from the grocery store and rushed across the parking lot. An itch between my shoulder blades had me checking back for any suspicious folk, or maybe the old man I'd disabled. There was no sign of him, or of anyone else paying special attention to Sadie and me.

I walked Sadie to the passenger side of the SUV and held the door until she was inside. Then I went around to the driver's side.

The hunched-over old-man demon stood beside the rear door.

I lifted my sword and prepared to extend the blade again. "If you don't want to die, you'd better run off now. You will get nothing from us."

The old man lifted his head and sniffed the air like a bloodhound catching a scent.

My stomach twisted.

"Your girl reeks of that wretched traitor," the old man rasped, his injured arm hanging limply at his side. "But I will let you be. For now. Tell Gorrath this: His days are numbered. The headsman's block still waits for him. His escape means nothing. Justice always finds its mark."

The man bobbed an awkward bow. Then he cradled his dangling arm and shuffled off around the rear of the SUV. I followed him to make sure he left. When I reached the back of the vehicle, there was no sign of him. He was gone.

I bent down to check beneath the truck and around the passenger side, but he wasn't there.

A chill ran down my spine as I climbed back into the driver's seat. "We have to get in touch with your aunt, and then we need to talk to Gorrath. There's something more going on here than a mistaken wild magic spell gone wrong."

"I'll text Aunt Rose about what happened. Can you stop somewhere and grab me a breakfast muffin or something? I'm starving again."

I forced a smile to show her it was all going to be fine. "Sure, I can do that."

I checked the mirrors to make sure we weren't followed out of the lot and let a bit of relief tint my mood.

Sadie, at least, seemed to be getting back to normal following her injury. Her healthy appetite was back. She always burned a lot of calories between soccer practice and the training sessions with Rose. The fight in the market must have reset something for her, and I was happy for that at least. She'd fought well. I had to get that girl a sandwich.

9

Rose

Warren's truck pulled up next to my Firebird in the parking lot at the recreation center. I'd asked him to meet up here. One of the county employees was an amateur demonologist we both knew from school. I hoped she might be interested in lending us her services in removing Gorrath from the ball.

The werewolf investigator met me as I got out of my car. "You sure you want me along on this, Rose?"

"Rosheen used to dabble in demonic history when we were both into the occult. I did it for training; she kept at it out of a morbid curiosity about demons and their interactions on this plane. We drifted apart after she tried summoning one right before we graduated."

"And you're afraid she won't want to do this just because you ask."

"That and the fact that she always liked you, Warren. You know she had a major crush on you during our junior year?"

"I remember. I also remember that she's a Naiad, and water fairies and werewolves rarely get along. Her mother was definitely against us going out after that first date. When I brought her daughter back, she met us at the door with a silver carving knife in her hand."

I chuckled. "Oh, yeah. You stayed pretty far away from Rosheen after her mom did that."

"You bet I did. Rosheen took it pretty hard, too. She wanted to defy her mother, and I refused to go along. I'm not sure she'll be all that sweet on me again after all these years."

"We have to try." I waved for Warren to follow. "Come on. I checked with her office. She's over here doing some work inside the rec center."

The building was extensive, and we entered through the double front doors and looked around. I'd never been inside before. Directly ahead, the foyer opened up into a large gymnasium and basketball court. Signs indicated several multipurpose rooms were to the right.

"Come on. She's in here somewhere." I entered the gym and spotted Rosheen right away, seated on the floor to the left with a pile of photos and folders beside her. A large bulletin board inside a glass case stretched along the wall above her.

Warren and I walked across the laminated wooden floor, the heels of my boots squeaking. Rosheen twisted around toward us.

I waved. "Hi, Rosheen. Remember me?"

"Rose? Is that you?" She climbed to her feet. "I don't think I've seen you since graduation. You've never come to any of the reunions." She smiled and gave Warren a big hug. "You, too, Warren. I can't believe you're both here again. It's almost like the old days."

"Almost," Warren said. He disengaged from the hug and grimaced a little when Rosheen turned away from him.

I shot him a stern look, then smiled and pointed at the collection of photos on the floor. "What's all this?"

"I'm updating the information on the bulletin board about upcoming events. We have our winter sports registration coming up in a month, along with several special seasonal events." She cocked her head to one side. "What are you doing here? I'm sure it's not the pottery class that's in a half hour."

"Actually, we came to see you."

"Me? What for?" She glanced back and forth between us.

"I need someone with a particular expertise, something you started learning back in school."

"I don't understand, Rose. What are you talking about?"

Warren sighed. "It's a demon thing. We're having a demon problem and thought of you."

Rosheen stiffened, a forced chuckle escaping her lips. "Demons? I mean, yeah, I studied them back in school, but that was ages ago. To be honest, I haven't touched that kind of magic in years."

I held up a hand. "It was me. Warren is only here because I asked him to come. If there was anyone else I could trust who was close by, I'd have contacted them. Everyone I know that can help with this kind of thing lives overseas."

"Rose, I don't know. It's been years since..." She trailed off, not finishing the sentence.

Warren inhaled deeply, his expression shifting from casual curiosity to something sharper. He took another slow breath, his brow furrowing. "That smell..." His eyes darted toward Rosheen. "It's subtle, but it's there. Brimstone."

My eyes went wide. "You've been close to a demon recently?"

Rosheen looked down at the floor, twisting her interlaced fingers.

I walked forward, seeing this was going to need a delicate touch. I reached for her hands and gave them a gentle squeeze. "Rosheen, are you in some kind of trouble? If you are, I can help. Warren, too. We can kick some serious ass between us."

Her breath hitched. A beat of silence passed as she spun the ring on her finger. "I... I can't talk about this here."

Her answer confused me. If she'd had recent contact with a demon and didn't need help, that meant she'd voluntarily encountered one. Had I made a mistake coming here?

"What are you mixed up with? Tell me. Now." I hated to be so stern, but demons weren't to be trifled with. We didn't want any running around the community, which was why we wanted to deal with the soccer ball as quickly as possible.

Rosheen took a step back. "No, you can't—you can't hurt him."

"Who? You're not making any sense." I reached out for her again.

Warren stepped up beside me and placed his hand on my arm, pressing down for me to lower it. "Rosheen, the brimstone smell is mixed closely with your own scent of rainwater and wildflowers." He paused and then added, "How long have the two of you been together?"

Rosheen's shocked expression shifted to worry. "It—it's going on fifteen years now. Oh, my gods. How did you know?"

"The scent." He pointed at her hand. "And the wedding ring made of intertwined red and white gold."

"Damn, Warren," I said. "That's why you're the best investigator around. I didn't even notice what the ring looks like."

Rosheen's fingers twisted the ring again. "You can't hurt him. He's not dangerous. I promise. He's a good husband and father."

"You had children with a demon?" The words slipped out before I could stop them, my voice sharper than I intended. My gut twisted. I had spent my life hunting demons, viewing them as nothing more than threats to be eliminated. And yet… here was Rosheen, standing before me, perfectly fine. Happy, even. Had I been wrong? Or was she just the exception?

"Yes." Rosheen's demeanor changed instantly. "And my children are wonderful, loving kids. You'd better not tell anyone about them or I'll—"

I held up a hand. "That wasn't fair of me. I have my own prejudices to deal with. Your secret is safe." I figured if there had been a problem demon running around Westminster, we'd have known it long ago. An idea occurred to me. "I do ask for some help in return for my silence. From you, and maybe your husband, too. I have a situation at home with my niece. Her Guardian and I ran into a little demon trouble with her, and we need some help."

Rosheen relaxed a little. "I suppose Bert and I could help. It would have to be discreet. No one knows about him. I tell everyone he's from Turkey because of his accent."

I hid a smile at the thought of Bert, the Turkish demon, hiding in plain sight here in town. "What's your number? I'll text you, and we can set up a time for you two to meet up so we can discuss the problem we're having. I think we all can be discreet about each other's situations."

Rosheen pulled a phone from her back jeans pocket. "Here. Enter your number. I'll text you, so you have mine."

I took her phone and put in my number. She sent a hello text and handed the phone to Warren to repeat the process. "We live up near Hampstead on a little farmette there. Bert grows organic produce for local restaurants and the farmer's market."

I snorted a chuckle. "Sorry, Rosheen. The thought of a demon selling organic carrots and sweet potatoes to suburban moms is making me laugh."

"Oh, believe me, we think it's a little funny, too. We've made a good life here together. We'd like to keep it that way." She fixed me with a stare, as if trying to read my thoughts.

"I swear on my family name, Rosheen. You'll have no trouble with me or Warren." My phone buzzed, and I looked down at the text that came in from Chip. I hid my alarm while I tugged at Warren's arm. "We should go so you can get back to work. I'd like to meet in the next day or so. Let's set it up."

"I'll wait to hear from you, Rose. You, too, Warren. It's been too long. It'll be nice to catch up some more. I've kept away from a lot of my high school friends since Bert came into my life."

I waved and hurried out to the parking lot.

Warren jogged along to catch up. "What's up?"

I handed him the phone to show him the text message. Then I fished into my pocket for the Firebird keys.

"Shit, Rose. A demon attack at the grocery store? That's not good. I'll meet you at the house after I swing by the store and see if there's anything I can learn about it."

"I was hoping you'd say that. Be thorough. It's bad enough we have one demon, but if there are more, then that means there's a—"

"—Portal," Warren finished. "Yeah. We need to lock this down. I'll let you know what I find out."

I jumped in, fired up the Firebird's engine, and sprayed gravel behind me as I pulled out of the lot to head back to Chip and Sadie at home.

10

Chip

I took a round-about route home from the grocery store, doubling back twice and taking unnecessary turns. A black sedan had been behind us for two blocks, but it peeled off at a gas station—coincidence or not? I checked the mirrors again.

Nothing.

My fingers tightened on the wheel. I was probably being paranoid. Probably. The whole demon encounter flustered me, though I was keeping it together on the outside so Sadie wouldn't notice.

"Uncle Chip, why are you driving in circles?" Sadie hooked a thumb over her shoulder toward a side street as we drove by. "We've missed a couple of chances to head home."

"Things are okay. I'm just not sure how the demons located us. I want to make sure no one follows us home." I checked the rearview and side-view mirrors again and nodded. "Yep, things are okay now."

"You said that twice. For future reference, if you want to keep me from worrying, you should avoid acting nervous yourself."

I pulled over to the curb and turned to face her in the passenger seat. "You're right. I'm sorry. You're old enough to help deal with this hiccup. You showed that back in the grocery store for sure."

"I can hold my own in a fight, Uncle Chip. You and Aunt Rose made sure I could take care of myself and the people I love."

"Yes, we did. It's just hard to switch out of Guardian mode and see you as more than the little girl I carried on my shoulders at the Renn Faire. You're growing up, and I hate that. It means I can't always keep you safe. But I'll try harder."

"What can I do to help?" Sadie asked, a big grin on her face.

"You watch the cars behind us and see if you can spot anyone following us. I'll start across town to our house for real now. If you see anything suspicious, tell me right away."

"Got it!" She gave me a big thumbs up and twisted in her seat to watch out the rear window while I drove.

Soon, I pulled into the driveway past Rose's Firebird and pushed the button to open the garage door. Rose stood with her arms crossed inside the garage as I pulled inside. I closed the door and shut off the engine.

She came around as I opened the door to get out. "What took you so long? I've been here for fifteen minutes." She looked around me at Sadie in the passenger seat. "Everyone all right?"

"Yes," Sadie said. "Uncle Chip was awesome, and I took care of one on my own, too."

"What happened?"

We stayed in the garage while I filled her in on our trip to the store and what had happened when Sadie spotted the first demon. It wouldn't do for Gorrath to hear this.

Sadie occasionally chimed in, but Rose listened without saying anything until we finished our story. "And that's all they said? That Gorrath was a fugitive, and they'd come to take him back?"

"That's pretty much it. They sensed his presence through Sadie. The house's wards must be proof against their ability to detect anything. That's good, but it also means she has to stay here until we solve this problem."

"Which I'm not doing." She crossed her arms. "As soon as the doctor says I can go back, I am going to school. The team needs me, and I don't want to miss so much school that I can't catch up."

I chuckled to myself. "You sure aren't anything like I was in school.

I would have been happy for an excuse to stay home. And we didn't have the internet when I was a kid."

Rose smiled. "She takes after her super-student mother there. That's Lily done all over."

"Come to think of it," I added. "That's Bobby, too."

Hearing the two of us talking about being like her parents brought a big grin to Sadie's face. She didn't have much memory of them, so she clung to these moments.

"So, what do we do with Gorrath now?" I asked. "We could be done with him. Maybe we turn him over to the demons in a neutral location?"

"There's still the connection to Sadie," Rose replied. "Until we deal with that and make sure there won't be unexpected side effects, we keep that ball safe."

Sadie put her fists on her hips and squared off opposite us in front of the SUV. "I'm not staying home for an indefinite time until Mr. Hitch uncovers a magical solution to this. I don't even feel Gorrath inside me anymore."

Rose said, "I've got a local demon expert coming to help. She promised she'd get with me in the next day or two."

"Two days?" Sadie's eyes narrowed. "I'm not staying home for two more days."

"You will if we need you to," I said. "Rose will get her friend to come as soon as she can, right?" I waited for Rose to answer.

"Absolutely. In fact, I will text her later this afternoon and see if she can meet tonight." Rose looked at Sadie. "How does that work for you?"

"Good, I guess. But I want to be there, too."

Sadie's request caught us both by surprise.

"You don't have to be there," Rose said. "We'll tell you everything we learn."

"You both want me to train all the time and learn to be the queen someday. Well, it's about time I learned about demons on my own. This won't be the last time I encounter them. I should be part of your plan."

I wanted to argue, but what could I say? Sadie had held her own against the demons at the grocery store. She'd trained for this since she could walk. And yet, part of me still saw the little girl who clung to my hand at her parents' funeral. I exhaled, shaking the image away. She wasn't that child anymore.

"She's not wrong, Rose. It's time."

Rose tapped her chin. "This situation is a little dicey. There's a confidentiality issue involved, and I'm not sure I'm allowed to reveal what I know to anyone else, let alone two more people."

Sadie crossed her arms. "I'm not changing my mind. This problem involves me. I need to be part of the solution."

Rose tensed, and I thought she might yell at Sadie right there in the garage. Then she relaxed. "You're right. It's time we let you grow up and join the family. You will be queen someday."

"Okay," I said. "That's settled. When do we meet this friend of yours? Can they come here?"

Rose shook her head. "No, I don't think they should come here. Gorrath is in there, and we don't know how much he can hear of what we say, even if we move him to another room."

"Then arrange for the three of us to go meet with them," I suggested. "We can go to a neutral location if they'd prefer."

Rose pulled out her phone. "I'll send her a text and see if she's around tonight."

"I'll see if Ellie can have Addy over to her house for dinner and homework tonight. That'll get him out of the house without bringing anyone else here to watch him. I don't want more people coming into contact with Gorrath if possible."

"Good thinking. Let me send this text and find out about tonight."

Rose tapped at her phone, and I dealt with something else on my mind. "Sadie, come with me. I know how we can isolate Gorrath so he doesn't listen in on everything we're doing while he's in the house. I also want to ask him about his friends at the market."

I walked into the kitchen from the garage and straight through the dining room to the family room, where the soccer ball remained perched on the sofa.

"Gorrath, we're back." I picked up the ball.

"Am I supposed to be impressed that you can come and go? I am completely stationary unless a child kicks me. What do I care?"

"You should care. We encountered other demons while we were out. They were very interested in tracking you down. Why are they so bent on finding you?"

"I have no idea. No one should know I am here as far as I'm aware. I was taken from the netherworld by force and awakened inside this cursed ball. Have you puny humans done anything at all to free me?"

I glared at the ball. "Careful with the puny comments, Gorrath. Right now you're a tiny leather sphere filled with air. I could drop kick you into the next county if I wanted."

A series of grumbles in a guttural language I didn't know followed. Gorrath finally said, "I was hasty in my remarks. Being cooped up in such a vessel is beneath me."

"You still haven't given me any solid answer on why there would be demons scouring our market looking for you."

"Why would they be looking for me?" Gorrath's voice rumbled inside the ball, too casual. "I have… enemies, certainly. Powerful ones. Perhaps they sensed something, a… disturbance when I was transported? Or maybe," he chuckled darkly, "you humans have bigger problems than me."

That answer made sense, but something in the tone didn't sound true to me. There might have been partial truth in his words, but he was hiding something.

"Well, all I know is we can't keep you here in plain sight in our family room. We're moving you to a more secure location." I motioned to Sadie, and she picked up the ball.

"At last, you see that I'm due certain courtesies. Where are we going? A throne room or audience chamber, perhaps?"

I laughed. "Oh, there's a throne all right." I walked to the stairs, and Sadie followed me around them and down the front hallway to the powder room. "Sadie, put him in the sink and run up and get that little Bluetooth speaker you got for Christmas."

While she ran off to do that, I went into the entertainment study and grabbed my old tablet. When Sadie returned, it was easy enough to connect to the speaker. I dialed up a streaming music app, and soon I had a classic rock playlist running.

"What is that infernal noise?" Gorrath shouted over the music. "I cannot hear myself think."

"That is the finest in rock and roll. I would think you demon types would be into the metal bands. Sit here and acquaint yourself with the finer parts of the genre."

Sadie and I left Gorrath in the sink with the speaker playing on the top of the toilet. I closed the door and walked away. "That will keep him from listening in on everything we do in this house while he's here. I don't trust him, Sadie. We have to be extra careful until we're rid of him."

"So, you're letting me come along tonight to the meeting with Aunt Rose's friend?"

"Yes," I replied. "You're right. It's time to include you as an adult in some things that affect this house."

Sadie's grin and bouncy step as she headed to the kitchen had me smiling, too. She was acting more like herself. I hoped she was almost back to normal after the concussion.

When we walked into the kitchen, Rose came in from the garage.

"The meeting's all set for tonight. We'll meet at their house. They want assurances and protections in place for their wellbeing. It's a touchy subject."

"Good, then we're all set," I said. "I'll get Ellie squared away to pick up Addy on her way back from getting Meredith at the high school. The middle school's on the way for her. She can keep him for the evening until we get back."

Ellie's kids were a little older than Addy. Her son, who everyone called Ace, was enrolled in the local community college, and her daughter, Meredith, was the same age as Sadie. Ellie had always treated both my kids like her own. Addy would feel at home over there for the evening, and it would keep him out of the house and away from Gorrath. With luck, we'd have a solution by the time we got home.

11

Rose

I let Chip drive us in his SUV. While on the way there, I filled him and Sadie in on the situation as much as I knew.

"So," Sadie said from the back seat. "She's really married to a demon? I wonder how that works. I mean, it would be dangerous, right?"

"Rosheen assures me that her husband is harmless and simply wants to live his life. I suppose there is such a thing as a passive and good demon. I just haven't met one yet."

"Hey, Rose," Chip said. "You're always telling me that ordinary people would misunderstand the existence of Unusuals in their communities if they knew about them. Maybe you're being the same way."

"Maybe, but you keep your sword handy on your belt, just in case."

We rode on in silence for the final few minutes and pulled up in front of a nondescript rancher home. The single-story house sat back from the road about two hundred yards, and we followed the winding driveway past several patches of tilled earth and gardens. This late in the fall, most of the harvest was done, but as we parked, our headlights lit up one patch still dotted by orange pumpkins.

"Until we make sure it's safe, Sadie, you stay behind Chip and me."

"I'm almost fully grown, Aunt Rose. It's not like I'm a kid anymore."

I glared at her, but she didn't back down. My surprise was hidden by the darkness. I calmed myself with long, slow breaths. "Fine. Just follow our lead. If either of us tells you to run, you book it."

She nodded, a huge grin on her face. Sadie hadn't won many arguments with me. Chip had adopted a saying that I fully agreed with: Never argue with toddlers or teenagers. I needed to remember that for next time if things went wrong here.

I walked up the brick path to the front door and raised my hand to rap on it. It popped open before I could knock.

A tall, muscular man stood inside. He wore a plaid cardigan sweater and jeans. He'd pulled his long black hair back in a low ponytail.

"You must be Rose." He extended a hand. "I'm Bert. Please, won't you all come in?"

I returned his firm handshake. His calloused hands felt normal, worn from working the land around their home. "Thank you. This is my brother-in-law, Chip Proctor. And this is my niece, Sadie."

Bert stepped back to let us in and closed the door behind us. "Rosh, honey. Our guests are here."

"I'll be right there. Just getting together the refreshments." Rosheen's voice came from deeper inside.

"Let's all sit in the living room over here." Bert led us to an area in front of a brick fireplace with a love seat, sofa, and recliner. The home seemed completely normal in every way. I sniffed at the air and didn't detect even a hint of brimstone.

Bert caught me testing the air. "I try to clean up after my days in the fields. You'd be surprised what a bit of Old Spice deodorant can cover up." He smiled, and I couldn't help but return it. He seemed very genuine.

Chip sat on the love seat beside Sadie. "So, Bert, I understand you and Rosheen met in high school?"

"After she was in high school. I did not attend with her, of course. I come from a place with a more unique system of education."

Chip smiled. "I'm not trying to catch you in anything. Just making conversation. It's not every day you meet a demon living in the community face to face."

Rosheen came in from their kitchen with a tray of glasses and a pitcher of what looked like apple cider. "This is Bert's own recipe for cider from our orchard. It's the best I've ever tasted. I think you'll like it." Rosheen set the tray on the coffee table and filled all the glasses before handing them around.

Sadie reached for one, and I asked, "The cider's not hard, is it?"

"No, though he has a peach brandy we grown-ups can sample later."

"I'm still working on that recipe," Bert said. "It's not quite ready for sharing, my dear."

"Nonsense," Rosheen said, sitting on the end of the sofa closest to the recliner he had settled into. I took a spot on the other end of the sofa.

Bert leaned forward after we'd all had a sip of cider. "Rosh tells me you're having a demon problem. I'm not sure what I can do for you, but if there's something I can do, I will help."

"We got attacked by them at the supermarket," Sadie blurted out.

Rosheen gasped. "Oh my goodness. In broad daylight?"

Bert shooshed her. "They attacked with no warning or signs of their arrival on this plane?"

"Maybe we should start at the beginning," I said and explained the events at the soccer game and bringing the ball home to discover Gorrath. Then Chip picked up with what had happened at the grocery store.

"And you're sure this possessed ball said it was Gorrath?" Bert asked. "That was the name it used?"

"Yes," Chip said. "And he's a bit of an asshole, if you don't mind me saying it."

"If it's really Gorrath, he's way more than that. Send him back. Right away. He's more dangerous than just about any other demons I knew back in the lower planes."

"What's so bad about him?" I asked. "Aren't all demons basically destructive? Present company excepted, of course."

"No offense taken. I'm most definitely not a normal demon. That's why I was so glad when Rosh invited me to stay here permanently. It hasn't been easy staying hidden, but it's been a better life than I could have hoped for in the underworld."

He reached out and gave Rosheen's hand a squeeze. She beamed a loving smile back at him.

"Um, I'm glad you found happiness, but what about Gorrath? What's so bad about him?"

Bert leaned back and picked up a pipe from the small table beside the recliner. He puffed on it without lighting it first. Wisps of smoke rose from the bowl.

"Gorrath isn't just another power-hungry demon. He doesn't just want chaos—he wants annihilation. No allegiances, no deals. If he's here now..." Bert let out a slow breath, fingers tightening on his pipe. "Then I don't think he was in hiding—I think he was trapped or imprisoned."

"Okay, so we know he's bad," Chip said.

"Not just bad," Bert said. "He's tried on several occasions to take over all the lower planes for himself. All to prepare for a total conquest of the middle plane, earth itself. His last attempt ended when all the various demon factions rallied against him, drove his forces back."

I tried to understand how this related to what had happened to Sadie. "If he was in hiding, then when Sadie pulled him here, it somehow exposed him again?"

"I'd say that sounds right." Bert pointed at Chip with the pipe. "You ran into warriors tasked with returning him to wherever he'd been before. We have very long memories. If they caught wind of him surfacing here in the mortal realm, they'd almost certainly come looking for him."

I liked nothing I was hearing. "What about his connection to Sadie? Is it possible to exorcise his influence from her?" I looked at Rosheen. "Could you perform the necessary rituals?"

"Maybe." Rosheen fidgeted on the sofa. "It's been a long time. I haven't dabbled in demonology since bringing Bert here fifteen years ago."

Bert shook his head. "Even if she was still versed in the rites, I'm not sure she'd have the power to do it alone. Gorrath has always been very powerful. He can extend his will over others from a great distance. You saw that in the fight at the soccer pitch."

"Well, if she can't do it alone, who can we get to help her?" I wasn't taking no for an answer. "We've got to get him out of her head and out of that ball. Then we have to either destroy him or send him back to where he came from."

Chip smiled. "We have the solution right in front of us."

"What?" I asked. "Chip, Rosheen just said she couldn't do it alone."

"Not her, at least not alone."

We all stared at Chip with no idea what he meant.

"Look. What if we just give Gorrath to those demons who are looking for him? In exchange, we could ask for their help in separating Gorrath's power from Sadie's."

Bert puffed at his pipe and blew a smoke ring. "That might just work. You'd have to find them, of course."

"I could do a simple locator spell, I suppose," Rosheen said. "They're not so hard, and there can't be that many demons around to confuse the signal. We know where Bert and Gorrath are. Anyone else would almost certainly have to be the rogues searching for the fugitive."

"Unless there's someone else we don't know of who has a demon for a spouse." Chip gave us all a big grin. "Come on. You know I'm right."

"There isn't anyone else like us," Bert said. "We'd have discovered them over the years, just like they'd have uncovered us. We demons have a sense for each other when we pass, even in disguise."

"Rosheen," I asked. "What do you need to do this spell?"

"I have some of the things I need in my old kit, but there are some components I'd have to get from a local herbalist or even a coven."

"I can help with that. You and I could go shopping tomorrow." I stopped when Chip's phone buzzed.

He frowned, pulling it from his pocket. He checked the screen.

"It's Ellie," he muttered, then answered as he walked away from the rest of us. "Hey, what's—"

He stiffened mid-step. His grip on the phone tightened.

"What do you mean, 'Addy is gone'?" He spun around and tapped the phone to turn on the speaker.

"—both gone. He and Ace went over to your house to pick up a video game he wanted to bring back here and play. I thought nothing of it until neither of them returned. They're gone. I went over to your house. The front door was wide open, and Ace's car was gone from our driveway."

"Ellie, this is Rose," I said. "Where did your son take Addy? Think!"

"I have no idea. He turned off the friends finder on his phone. I can't see where he is."

I pulled out my phone and tried to track Addy. His phone was off, or he'd turned off tracking, too.

"We'll be right there." I started to the door. "Chip, we have to hurry."

"It's Gorrath," he said, falling in step beside me. Sadie trotted up behind us.

"If Gorrath took the boy, he must have taken control somehow," Bert said. "Is this Ace an Unusual?"

"No," I said. "Plain old human. He'd have no resistance to demonic control. If Addy brought him into the house, it wouldn't take much for a demon to take over."

"Rosh and I will come along and help you look. I should be able to help sense their location if we get close." Bert set down his pipe on a ceramic holder beside his chair.

"Bert, honey, this could expose you to those who don't know you're here."

"I don't care. If these boys are in danger, I have to help."

Chip and Sadie bolted through the front door.

I wasn't far behind. I shot one last look at Bert and Rosheen. "If you're coming, move. Now. We don't have time to wait."

I didn't know what Addy was thinking by taking Ace over to the house alone. Once this was over, I was going to have a long talk with that boy about planning ahead.

12

Chip

I slid to a stop in the driveway inches from the garage, my eyes on the open front door. Sadie jumped out and ran ahead of us inside before we could stop her.

Ellie walked across the street from her house.

I waved at our neighbor. "Rose, go with Sadie inside and see what you can find. I'll deal with Ellie."

The short, redheaded housewife wrung her hands while she walked up the driveway to where I stood. "Chip, I don't know what that boy was thinking, running off with Addy that way. I promise you, we will have a long, stern talk with him when he comes back."

I knew it wasn't Ace's fault, and I didn't want this coming between Ellie and me. She was a good woman and had always helped when we needed it.

"Addy's old enough to know better than to run off like this, too. We can both have a chat with our boys once they're home. What kind of car does Ace drive? Maybe it's got a GPS the police can track."

Ellie shook her head. "I don't think so. It's an old beater we helped him buy just to go to school and work. It doesn't have much in the way of bells and whistles."

I frowned. I'd hoped GPS would help us find them.

"Steve left right away to look for them," Ellie said. "I just feel awful, Chip."

"Don't. I'm serious. Boys will be boys. Why don't you head home and stay there in case they come back? Between Rose and I, we can go out and look around, too." I nodded at the minivan pulled up out front. "We have some other friends to help, too. We'll find them."

Ellie returned to her house across the street. I waved to Bert and Rosheen, and they followed me inside.

Bert sniffed at the air as soon as he entered. "I can sense another of my kind was here. If that was Gorrath, I'll know it if we get close to their location."

"Good," Rose said. She gripped her sheathed sword in her left hand and pointed outside. "The ball is gone. Gorrath definitely has them. Sadie and I will go looking in the SUV with you, Chip. Bert and Rosheen can follow in their van."

Sadie walked out with a short-handled battle axe in hand and stood by Rose.

"What are you going to do with that thing?" I asked.

"If we get attacked by demons again, I want more than soup cans handy to defend myself. Aunt Rose said it was okay."

Rose nodded. "Don't worry. I won't let her chop anyone by accident. Now, back to Addy. Where would Gorrath take them once he had control? He has to have a plan of some sort."

Bert opened his mouth and then shut it.

"What?" I asked.

"There's an old buried temple outside of town. I sensed it long ago while driving around. I've never been there, but I got a sense it might still be active. Gorrath may have been able to sense its power as well. I'd be careful, though. If it is still active, there must be a cabal of worshipers energizing it."

Rosheen gripped Bert's arm. "If you get too close, they might expose you, honey. Maybe you should just give them the directions."

"No, I'm part of this community. I won't shirk my duty to protect those who live here."

I patted Bert on the shoulder. "Good man. It's good to have people in this world like you. Take Rosheen in your van and lead the way. We'll follow in my SUV."

Sadie followed Rose and me over to the truck and climbed in the back with her axe. I shook my head. She had grown in recent years, but I never saw how much she resembled her aunt until now. She'd become quite the impressive young woman.

We followed Burt through town and down Route 27 into an area of rolling farmland with a scattering of housing developments here and there. He turned off onto a winding country road, guiding us into a thickly wooded area. As we neared a gravel drive leading back into the forest, he pulled to the right side.

Burt got out and walked back to the driver's side of the SUV. I wound my window down as he approached.

"The old temple has to be back in there." He pointed into the trees. "I think this gravel track leads to it, but it's dark, and I don't think we should just drive in there with our headlights blazing. They'll see us coming."

"You're sure there are people back there now?"

Bert nodded. "I can sense the power of their rites. It's not the residual glow I'd get from a dormant shrine. There's definitely something happening back there."

Rose popped open her door. "Then we go now. Addy's back there, and we don't have any reason to believe they'll be nice just because he's a kid. These are demon worshipers." She drew her sword and tossed the scabbard onto the passenger seat.

"Okay, let's do this then." I opened my door and climbed out. I wasn't sure we had to go in with weapons drawn, so I opted to keep my sword's hilt where it was clipped to my belt.

Sadie got out behind me. She hefted her axe and grinned.

Rose frowned. "This is deadly serious, Sadie. You stay back behind your uncle and me. Got it?"

She got an enthusiastic head bob in reply.

Rosheen had gotten out of the minivan. Worry creased her brow. "Be careful, honey. I'll stay here with the cars." She held up her phone. "Call if you want me to drive down the lane."

Bert smiled. "I'll be back before you know it. Just keep watch." He led the three of us down the gravel lane.

We walked in the darkness. I had activated my dark sight using my shark's tooth charm. The bit of moonlight that filtered down through the tree branches gave an eerie bluish glow to everything. Sadie and Rose could see well in the dark, too, being Fae. Apparently, Bert could as well, since he set a fast pace.

After about three minutes, rhythmic chanting came from up ahead. I tried to guess the number of people we might expect based on the voices, but I couldn't isolate them enough. It was more than just a few, though.

Bert stopped. "We're close, and the power is ramping up. They're nearing the pinnacle of their rites. I can sense it."

"Then we have to hurry," Rose said. "Addy could be in danger." She rushed past down the lane.

Sadie brandished her axe and followed. I had little choice but to run after the pair. Bert fell in right behind me.

The dim glow of firelight lit a ruined house without a roof. The stone foundation and most of the walls rose from the ground. A cluster of four parked vehicles lay off to the left. I spotted Ace's old F-100 pickup truck. Inside the ruin, shadows reflected on the walls and danced around in time with the chanting.

Rose slowed to a crouching walk and approached the nearest stone wall, rising enough to peer through a vacant window. Without looking back, she waved us forward to where she hid.

"There's five in there, including Ace," Rose whispered. "Addy's tied up and lying on the floor against the far wall."

"What's the plan?" I asked.

"You and Sadie circle around back and be ready to come in to cover Addy from that direction. I'll give you time to get into position before I move."

I nodded and waved to Sadie to follow me. We bent over to stay below the line of windows and ran to the corner of the old building. I peeked around it and then darted past the open frame of a doorway. Sadie followed right behind. A minute later, I had turned the far corner and was in position beside another doorway with three stone steps leading up to it.

I checked on Sadie, and her wild expression startled me. "Get to Addy and untie him. That's it. Okay?"

Her sapphire blue eyes met mine, and she nodded, gripping the haft of the axe and holding it right in front of her.

Rose's voice shouted over the chanting. "That's enough of that. Everyone step away from the altar."

The chanting halted, and I didn't hesitate. The worshipers would be looking at Rose and not back here. I unclipped the hilt from my belt and extended the meter-long blade with a thought. Then I ran up the steps and inside the fire-lit interior.

Crude stone statues of what were probably supposed to be demons stood at intervals along the walls on both sides of the single room. Far to the left was an altar made of the same stones as the walls. Beside it stood Ace Johnson, his face lit up by the fire in the center of the room. Before him on the altar was the soccer ball containing Gorrath.

Four people in gray and red robes stood around the fire with their arms raised. All had twisted around to face away from my entrance.

Rose stood in an open window frame with her sword gleaming in the firelight. Bert had circled partway around and stood in the first doorway I'd passed.

Addy was seated against the wall to our left, bound. I pointed, and Sadie rushed past me to her little brother.

Everyone had frozen for a second. I didn't know if I should attack the people around the fire or not.

By the altar, Gorrath's voice sounded from Ace's mouth. "Intruders! Release the guardians like I showed you."

With one voice, the four around the fire shouted a word in an ugly, guttural language. A hideous groaning of stone rubbing together emanated from all around. It took me a second to realize it was the six statues spaced along the two long walls of the building.

The stone statues shuddered violently, fractures spider-webbing across their surfaces. Then, in a sickening cascade of cracking and snapping, chunks of rock peeled away like molted skin, revealing the hulking creatures beneath. Their twisted forms were still half-fused with stone, jagged remnants of their prison jutting from their shoulders like crude armor.

One of them took a lumbering step forward. The mucus dripping from its claws hit the dirt—and the earth hissed and smoked where it landed.

Bert called out, "They're Radacks. Ware their bite!"

I didn't need the warning after seeing what their spittle did.

Across from me, Rose leaped forward at the back of the nearest demon. Her blade glowed with blue fire. She swung it down at the Radack's back. Her sword cut deep.

The demon staggered forward. It didn't fall, though. Despite the gaping wound on its back, it twisted around and swiped at Rose with two clawed hands.

I decided if slashing didn't work, maybe thrusting would. I lunged forward at the side of the nearest Radack. My sword pierced the thick hide with some effort but didn't drive as deep as I'd hoped. White fire glowed along the length of my sword, and smoke emerged from the area around the steel where it entered the demon's armpit.

The demon howled and tried to trap my blade by clamping down with its arm. I twisted my wrist, as Rose had taught me. The sword pulled free, opening the wound further as it slid out.

I ducked under an awkward swing at my head from my opponent and spared a glance back at Sadie. She'd freed Addy. They stood back-to-back, and Addy had picked up a rock in each hand to use as crude weapons.

When the nearest Radack reached for her, Sadie swung her axe hard and lopped off a few clawed fingers. Her axe glowed with the same sapphire blue as her eyes, which were also glowing.

I grunted when a clawed hand slashed at my shoulder. Three gashes opened up through the tears in my coat.

The demon tried to catch me with its other hand, but I stepped back, away from it.

I swung the sword two-handed with all my might at the demon's neck. The white fire hissed, and the blade cut nearly all the way through.

The demon let out a gurgling cry and clutched at the open wound in its neck. A second later, the fire went out of its eyes, and it crumpled to the ground.

I hardly noticed the worshipers fleeing through the broken rocks at the far corner, running for their cars. Before I had fully recovered, another demon leaped forward at me.

I dodged under the attack, and the demon sailed over my head into the bonfire at the center of the room, scattering the stacked logs. Ace darted past me, holding Gorrath the soccer ball in front of him like a trophy. In a desperate move, I swept out with my left leg toward Ace.

He tripped, spilling forward and launching the ball toward the fleeing demon worshipers. One stopped and reached for it.

The soccer ball hung suspended in mid-air, glowing an eerie red as if savoring its freedom.

"You've only delayed the inevitable," Gorrath's voice rasped from within.

The cultist's eyes rolled back in his head, and with a burst of unnatural speed, sprinted into the night before I could even react.

I cursed, then spotted the advancing Radack coming at me. I tucked and rolled forward just in time to avoid the demon's return from its encounter with the fire.

Burning embers dotted its coarse hide where the tufts of hair emerged. It didn't seem fazed by the fire at all. The Radack roared and charged after me.

I rolled to my feet and braced with my sword stretched out. The impact with the charging demon slid me back a few feet along the dirt floor.

My blade pierced the demon's chest all the way to the hilt as the demon pulled me into a crushing embrace.

I twisted my face away from the dripping fangs while I brought up a knee in between us. With all the effort I could muster, I shoved with one leg.

The impaled Radack fell backward, my sword sliding free from its chest. It came to rest on its back and twitched a few times before it went still.

Sadie let loose her battle cry as she spun completely around with her axe. Her glowing blue blade trailed fire and swept all the way through the torso of the Radack lunging at her.

Its two halves fell apart, with the upper half toppling over onto Sadie. The bottom half took two steps, then collapsed.

The heavy torso trapped Sadie until Addy tugged it off her.

I breathed a sigh of relief when she rose, wild blue fire in her eyes. She stared around the room, her breaths coming in heaving gasps, looking for another enemy.

All six of the statue guardians were down. Rose had dispatched the one she'd attacked. In the corner, a nine-foot-tall demon with red skin stood over two more Radack bodies.

In the dim firelight, the towering demon turned toward me, his crimson skin gleaming, the last remnants of his human disguise reduced to tatters hanging off his monstrous frame.

My grip on my sword tightened instinctively. My brain screamed demon, but my gut warned me to hold back.

"Bert?" I asked, just to be sure.

The giant demon gave me a sharp-toothed grin. "I haven't had a good fight in many, many years."

I let out a slow breath. "Good to know you're still on our side."

"That was beyond exhilarating."

I slumped against the wall, my chest heaving. My sword felt heavier than it should as I retracted the blade back into its hilt.

Rose wiped a streak of black demon ichor from her face, her breath coming in ragged gasps.

Sadie, still gripping her axe, wobbled slightly. Addy reached out and steadied her.

We'd won the fight.

But we'd lost the war.

My eyes met Rose's.

This wasn't over.

13

Rose

I flicked my sword down and to the right to fling off the droplets of demon ichor and the blood that still clung to the blade. Chip and I took a moment to assess the situation and nodded to each other.

Four quick steps took me to Addy's side. "Are you okay?" I gripped his shoulder and turned him around to check him for injuries or signs of abuse.

"I'm fine, Aunt Rose. That was an awesome fight. I've never seen real demons in person before."

I took a step back and stared at him. He was almost as tall as I was, but I still managed to look down at him. "That's only because you did something really dumb. Do you know what it was?"

Addy swallowed hard, glancing at the demon bodies again before looking away. "I—I took a mundane into the house too close to Gorrath."

"Is that a question or a statement?" I pressed.

His shoulders slumped. "A statement." He let out a shaky breath. "I thought it was no big deal. But then… I mean, what if Ace had gotten possessed permanently? Or what if Gorrath had used me for something worse?"

His voice wavered on the last part.

I softened a little. "That's why we train, Addy. You have to think ahead. You're not just some kid in this fight—you're Sadie's champion."

He nodded, more solemn now. "I won't mess up like that again."

"Well, I think you've learned your lesson. Help me get Ace to his feet." The teenager had groaned and made a few unsuccessful attempts to get up off the ground.

Addy and I bent down and pulled the neighbor boy upright. He wobbled a little before he finally got his balance back.

"Hey, Miss Rose." His wide eyes took in the location and the bodies around on the floor. "Wh-what happened?"

"Do you remember anything?"

"I remember going over to your house with the little guy here, then I heard loud music playing down the hallway. After that, well, it gets really hazy. I mean, unless you believe in talking soccer balls." He gave an embarrassed chuckle, and his face flushed. Then he took in the demon bodies and parts lying around him and squeezed his eyes shut.

"That's it. Keep them closed until we get you out of here." I motioned for Chip to come over.

He clipped the collapsed sword hilt to his belt and shoved a hand under Ace's arm, lifting him up a little when he wobbled again. I took the other side, and together we walked him out of the stone building until we stood on the gravel track outside.

Headlights lit us up as a vehicle approached down the lane. It was Rosheen in the minivan. She pulled up next to us and put down the passenger window, leaning over to see us. "Is Bert okay? I saw all the cars leave and then nothing."

"Bert's fine," Chip said. "Just a little taller and red."

"Really? He hasn't slipped into his actual form in a long time."

"We needed the help. Rose and I would have been lost without his assistance."

I didn't know about that, but I knew Chip was trying to reassure the woman. She'd helped us out and deserved that much, at least.

Bert came out of the building with Sadie beside him. He had

reverted to his human form and approached in the torn pants and shirt wrecked by his transformation. His feet were bare, too.

"Hey, babe. We had a bit of a scuffle, but we got the boys back."

"I see that. I'm glad you could help. So what do we do now? Is that it?"

I shook my head. "First, we get Ace on his way home." I pointed at the lone pickup truck parked under the trees beside the temple building. "Are you well enough to drive home? Your parents are very worried about you."

"I think I'm good." Ace dug into his pocket and pulled out his keys. "But what do I tell them about what happened here? They'll never believe what I saw in there."

Chip said, "I'll send your mom a text telling her that Rose and I worked it out with you, okay? We know it wasn't your fault, but you will probably want to keep all this to yourself."

"You don't have to tell me twice."

"Good. Now go back up the lane and turn right on the road, and it'll take you back to Route 27. You can find your way home from there, right?"

"I can. Thank you, Mr. Chip." He walked over to his truck, got in, and drove away back up the lane to the main road.

Once his red taillights faded into the darkness, I said, "We still need to get that ball. It's linked to Sadie somehow, and I don't like it."

"You said he arrived in some sort of portal," Rosheen said. "That means you won't just need an exorcism, you'll also need someone to seal the opening closed after you remove him from the ball."

"Can you do the exorcism?" I asked.

"Probably, if Bert helps with the research ahead of time. There are a lot of things that have to occur in the rites to make it happen."

"Okay, let me know if you need anything or anyone to help you. This is priority one."

"Not exactly," Chip said. "We don't have Gorrath anymore."

"He's a force for chaos. He won't be able to hide for long. Besides, I think he needs Sadie as much as we need him."

"I don't like the sound of that," Sadie said. "That means he'll come back for me."

"He has to. We have to be ready to go when he does."

Addy shivered and wrapped his arms around himself. He was in jeans and a T-shirt, and it was chilly out. I took off my leather jacket and wrapped it around his shoulders.

"Okay, we can't do anything else out here. I'll send a message to Warren to have a crew come out and dispose of the demon bodies. Let's get home and figure out the next steps there."

Chip nodded and reached out to shake Bert's hand. "Thanks for everything. We're in your debt. I don't take that lightly."

I winced. It wasn't good to owe a demon a favor, even one who was reformed. "Bert was just doing a good deed for the deed's sake, right?"

Bert smiled. "Yes, yes. No debt is owed to me or mine by thee or thine."

I recognized the old formal speech for what it was. "Thank you, Bert. Let's pile into the van and hitch a ride back out to the SUV on the road."

Bert opened the side door, and the two kids piled in, followed by Chip and then me. Bert got into the passenger seat, and Rosheen took us away from the demon temple.

After we got in our own vehicle, the chatter from the back seat provided plenty of entertainment for Chip and me up front. Addy and Sadie talked about the rescue and the battle with the demons. Their animated voices had both of us grinning despite the seriousness of the situation. It was good to have our family back together again.

During a lull in the kids' conversation, I broke in. "Addy, did you hear anything about what Gorrath had planned next?"

Addy shifted uncomfortably. "They weren't gonna sacrifice me or anything… but from the way Gorrath talked, he needed a huge crowd. More people meant more power to bring his army here."

"An army?" Chip echoed. "Like, how many?"

Addy hesitated. "Thousands. Maybe tens of thousands."

A cold weight settled in my stomach. "That's not just a battle. That's an invasion."

Chip exhaled. "Westminster isn't ready for something like that."

"Nowhere is," I muttered. "Having an army of demons show up in the middle of Westminster would cause a major incursion of the kind not seen since the dark ages."

"How did people beat them back then?" Chip still wasn't as versed in Unusual history as he could have been. "I mean, we have modern weapons and tanks and stuff now. I have to believe we'd defeat an army of demons pretty easily."

"Think about what you encountered in the grocery store with Sadie. If they could all assume human form and mingle with the general population, how would you figure out which people you could kill on sight?"

"Oh," he said. "I didn't realize that's what would happen."

"Ultimately, everyone had to rely on the powers from the higher planes to assist us. We had the Eldara warriors mixed into our armies. They had the divine power to command demons to revert to their natural forms. It was a bloody mess for a while until they all were exposed."

"Eldara?" Chip asked. "Those are angels, right?"

"Yes, they're what you would call angels. The problem is, the gods of the higher planes and the demon lords of the lower planes made a truce and agreed to never fight a war like that on earth again. It keeps both sides from major incursions like the one Gorrath is planning."

One of Chip's eyebrows went up. "But wait, if Gorrath shows up and breaks the truce, won't the angel warriors be able to come back, too?"

"There are some who remained here on earth performing various missions of good and kindness, but the vast warrior legions returned home. I've heard of a few who return from time to time. There were rumors about a Valkyrie hanging around Elk City a few years back."

Chip's eyes widened. "A real, winged, battle-maiden Valkyrie?"

"If the stories were true, yes." I tapped my chin, thinking. "A single Valkyrie fought entire demon legions in the old wars. If we could find her…"

"Sounds like we need to start making some calls." Chip grinned. "Gibbie lives in Elk City."

"I can't see Gibbie running in the high society circles of a Valkyrie."

"I know you don't think much of him. If there was such a thing as a vampire nerd, it would be Cousin Gibbie. But maybe he knows someone who knows a guy who could track down this winged warrior maiden. We won't know if I don't ask."

Chip left it there since we'd just pulled into the driveway. It was late, and the kids were both tired after the ordeal at the temple. Chip said, "Head right inside and get cleaned up. Addy, you especially. You haven't showered in a while, and I can tell."

Sadie laughed. "Ha, I told you, you stunk, bro."

"What are you laughing at?" Addy pointed at Sadie's head. "There's demon guts all caked in your hair."

"Ewww." Sadie's hand went up and probed at the sticky mess. "Dibs on the shower first." She jumped out of the SUV and raced inside.

"Uncle Chip?" Addy whined. "She'll be in there forever now."

"Don't worry about it," Chip said. "You can use mine in the master suite. Go. You do smell a little."

Addy lifted an arm to sniff underneath, shrugged, and went inside.

I laughed. "What are we going to do for entertainment when those two grow up and move out?"

"Oh, I'm never letting them leave. I've decided they will stay here and live with me forever."

"Little birds gonna fly eventually, Chip. It's the circle of life."

He smiled. "Don't act like you won't miss them, too."

He followed me around to the front of the SUV by the open garage door. "Yeah, but they'll always make time when their cool aunt comes by to visit. You've got that dad energy going on. Nobody wants to live with their 'rents forever."

"I guess you're right. We'll have to make the most of the time left. See you tomorrow, Rose."

"Yeah, I've got to check in with Warren and Hitch. They both better have some answers for me." I waved and walked down the driveway.

As I slid into the Firebird, I let out a slow breath. The night's battle had left a dull ache in my muscles, but it wasn't just physical exhaustion weighing on me.

We'd won the battle, but Gorrath was still out there.

I rested my head against the steering wheel for a second, just long enough to feel the tension settle into my bones. Then, with a shake of my head, I turned the key.

No time for rest. Tomorrow, we hunted demons.

14

Chip

I was glad the next day was a Saturday so we could all sleep in. I needed it after the battle the night before. Still, I was surprised to find I was the first one up when I stumbled downstairs at ten thirty the next morning. I appreciated the relative quiet for a while and started a pot of coffee to enjoy some time alone for a change.

Ten minutes later, I sat at the kitchen table with my phone in one hand and a mug of Columbia's finest dark roast in the other. It wasn't to last, though. I heard a shouted exchange from upstairs, followed by running feet thumping down to the first floor. The kitchen door swung open, and Sadie chased Addy into the kitchen.

They made one complete orbit of the table before I shouted, "That's enough!"

Addy slid to a stop beside me. "I'm sorry. I told her it was an accident."

Sadie stood across the table in shorts and a tank top, her hands clenched into fists at her side. "He's lying. He's always lying."

"Now, that's not fair," I said. "Addy, what did you do?"

"I was washing my hands in the bathroom, and I accidentally knocked her jar of face cream on the floor."

"It shattered and splatted all over the floor. It was a gift from Aunt Rose. She brought it back from France."

"He said he was sorry."

"He's lying. When does he remember to wash his hands after he goes to the bathroom? He's a pig. All boys are."

I didn't want to take her side, but she wasn't wrong. It was unusual for Addy to be anything approaching hygienic. Still, I couldn't have them at each other's throats all morning.

"Addy, get your phone and text Aunt Rose. Ask her where you can get more of the face cream."

He dug his phone from his pajama pants pocket and smiled as if he'd won a prize.

"While you're at it, tell her you're paying for it with your allowance."

Addy frowned. "But it's expensive."

"Then you'll have to do extra chores to make up for it. Send the message and go empty the dishwasher for a start."

Addy tapped on his phone for a second and then shuffled over to the dishwasher. He grumbled something I couldn't make out. I let it drop. Sadie, on the other hand, wasn't finished.

An actual snarl erupted from her. "He's not sorry. It was a special gift that can't be replaced. You should make him pay."

"I did make him pay, Sadie. And watch your tone or you'll get some extra chores, too."

Her voice deepened into Gorrath's growl. "I will get revenge on the boy and the rest of you, too." She stomped her foot, sending out a shower of magical, glowing red sparks from beneath her heel. Then she stormed out of the kitchen and back upstairs.

I was about to send Rose a message about what had just happened when I noticed Addy staring at the floor on the other side of the table.

"What are you looking at, bud?"

"Uh, Uncle Chip. That's not good." He pointed at a spot blocked from my view by the table's edge.

I got up and leaned over the table. A tiny circle of red glowing dots expanded until it was nearly a foot across. A puff of acrid smoke wafted up through the opening, making me wrinkle my nose. I was staring down into a fiery mountainous landscape with rivers of lava and bat-winged demon birds flying by.

"Addy, stand back." I waited for it to grow larger, but it stopped expanding. I grabbed my phone from the table and was about to snap a photo to send to Rose when small, red-skinned fingers ending in tiny, pointed claws gripped the edge of the hole.

A horned head popped up, and the little demon's mouth opened to show a row of needle-pointed teeth. It screeched, and its wings unfurled as it launched itself upward, flapping around the kitchen ceiling. It was about the size of a chicken.

"Oh, man, that's an imp," Addy said. "That's not good."

"Why? I can take care of a little thing like that." I prepared to use my Guardian barrier spell to press the little beast into the corner of the ceiling.

"Aunt Rose said they always travel in packs. See?" He pointed down at the hole, where two more imps fought to climb through at the same time.

On pure instinct, I stomped down toward the pair, who were struggling halfway through the hole. I changed my mind at the last instant when I remembered I was barefooted. Instead, I pressed down with my Guardian barrier over the opening.

The transparent magical field, shaped in my mind to be about the size of a trash can lid, squashed down and trapped the flailing pair trying to climb through. They both let out a string of shrieks and guttural words in their tiny, high-pitched voices. Other hands squeezed past their squirming bodies and pressed on the barrier. There were a lot more imps trying to get through.

I'd forgotten about the single imp who'd made it into the kitchen. Addy shouted a warning right before a sound like a buzz saw erupted right behind me. It landed on my shoulders, straddling my neck, and dug its tiny needle-like claws into my scalp.

"Yowwww!" I reached back with both hands to rip the attacking imp from my shoulders.

It chittered a jeering laugh at me and launched backward into the air, flapping its wings and darting left and right against the ceiling. I reached up to grasp the dodging mini-demon.

"Uncle Chip! The hole."

Damn, I'd forgotten about the imps trying to escape through the portal in the floor. Before I could raise my barrier again, four more imps climbed through and launched themselves inside the kitchen.

I grabbed my insulated mug from the table and threw it sidearm at one imp as it hovered in the corner. The mug caromed off its horned noggin.

The little creature shook its head back and forth twice before it locked its eyes on mine. Then it launched out straight at me.

I yelped and dove over backward in a poor attempt at a back handspring move I'd seen Rose do once. I crashed into the countertop, jarring my shoulder to the bone. My shoulder ached when I tried to move it, but it didn't feel like it was broken.

A fiery sphere the size of a golf ball sizzled past my face. I ducked down just in time to avoid three more like it. Three of the imps stood on the kitchen table and wound up like major league pitchers ready to launch more fireballs my way.

"Addy, how the hell do we beat them? The cup I threw didn't even phase it."

"Cold steel or iron." Addy ducked down behind the granite countertop, barely avoiding a pair of fireballs aimed at his face.

My sword was upstairs, so cold steel was out. Then my gaze fell on the stove across the kitchen.

I dove forward, rolled up, and grabbed the cast-iron frying pan just in time to swat back two of the fire orbs. It was like playing pickle ball at the YMCA. I hit one of the flying imps with a return shot. It yelped and fell from the table, a hole burned through its thin wing membrane.

At least no more were coming through the hole. But I couldn't count on it staying that way. I had to deal with the five imps here in the kitchen quickly.

I dodged three more of their flaming balls, then I charged straight at the trio atop the table.

Two rocketed away before I got there, but the last one fled a bit too late.

I batted at it with a full forehand swing. The frying pan connected with a satisfying crunch. A flash of magic flared from my shark charm, and the power ran down my arm into the iron pan.

The imp let out a choked-off screech and fell away from the pan—only it was now a perfect imp-sized statue made of stone.

"Yes!" I shouted.

Addy called out, "Behind you."

I ducked and spun, swinging backhand as one of the flying imps zoomed past my head. The frying pan caught it from behind, swatting it into the wall.

Another little imp statue lodged in the drywall and hung there with only its legs hanging out.

The hole to the netherworld was at my feet, and I needed to close it before more came through. I shrugged and flipped the round table over, dumping the remains of breakfast across the floor. The heavy table landed over the opening to hell. I didn't think any more imps on the far side would be strong enough to move it.

"Okay, you little punks. It's time to meet my friend." I waved the frying pan over my head.

The three imps circling the light fixture on the ceiling shrieked and yowled in fear. They scattered as I charged.

Two dove toward the stove away from me. The other was the one with the damaged wing. It tried to dodge past me, but I was faster.

Whunnnng went the frying pan. Scratch one more demonette.

After that, it was a frenzy of dodging fireballs and swinging cookware. I chased the last two imps around the kitchen, the frying pan swiveling. They were fast and clever, working in tandem. One dodged, while the other hurled fireballs. My bathrobe now had more holes than fabric.

I faked a lunge. The nearest imp darted sideways—right into my swing. *Whunnng!* The frying pan met its mark, and another tiny stone statue tumbled across the counter.

The last imp screeched in panic and dove for the hole, trying to lift the overturned table.

I launched forward, slamming the pan down just as its claws scraped at the wood. One final, muffled *whump*—and that was that. I lay there on the floor with my chest heaving while I tried to catch my breath.

"You're not going to cook with that anymore, are you?"

I rolled over and looked up at Addy's smiling face. "Sure, why not? We don't have to tell anyone it's my imp-whomping frying pan."

That set him to giggling. He started picking up the imp statues and set them on the island.

I pulled out the one stuck in the wall and then took in the entire kitchen. There were scorch marks on all the walls and a few spots on the ceiling. Some of the cabinets smoldered.

I ran to the sink and grabbed the spray hose. With a flick of my hand, I turned on the water to full power and sprayed the smoking spots until the smoldering stopped. I shook my head. It was going to take more than just a fresh coat of paint to fix this.

"Addy, you pick up the breakfast dishes here while I go up and check on your sister. Be careful you don't move the table. We probably need to call your aunt and see if Mr. Hitch or someone else can come and close up that hole."

"I can text her if you want?"

"Yeah, you do that. Tell her to come as soon as she can. I'll be upstairs with Sadie."

I left Addy in the kitchen. It wasn't until I was halfway up the steps that I realized I was still carrying the frying pan. I set it on the top of the bookshelf in the upstairs hallway outside Sadie's room.

"Sadie, hon. Can I come in?" I tapped on the door with a knuckle.

"It's not like I can stop you."

I swallowed the angry answer welling up inside me. What happened was Gorrath's doing and not hers. I had to remember that.

"I know what happened downstairs wasn't your fault."

The door opened, and I was face-to-face with my niece. "I heard shouting down there. What were you and Addy doing after I left?"

"Fighting the imps you let into the kitchen."

Sadie's eyes widened. "What? I didn't—"

"I know you didn't do it on purpose. You were channeling Gorrath again. But he used your power to open a small portal on the kitchen floor, and a group of imps came through."

She lowered her eyes to take in my scorched, holed bathrobe. "You okay?"

"I'll be fine. We found a solution. Your aunt will be here soon to deal with the rest of the situation. I want to know what you were feeling when you came down this morning. We need to understand what that demon is doing to influence you, so you don't let this happen again."

Sadie's shoulders sagged, and she hugged her arms around herself. "I don't really know. I woke up in a haze. Then I got angry with Addy, and then you—" Her breath hitched. "It all built up so fast. And then he was there. I could feel him pushing into my mind, like he was—" She swallowed. "Like he was waiting for me to lose control."

She let out a breath. "I don't know how long I was... not me. I think I was still there, somewhere, but I couldn't fight him."

"Could you hear him?" I asked gently.

She hesitated. "Not words, exactly. More like... laughter." Her fingers clenched the blanket in her lap. "He liked it. He wanted me to lose control."

That sent a chill up my spine. Gorrath was waiting for this. And next time, he wouldn't stop at a handful of imps.

She blinked hard, her fists clenching in her lap. "I let him in. It's my fault."

I sat beside her and squeezed her shoulder. "It's not your fault, kiddo. He's a parasite. But we're going to make sure he never does this again."

"I'm sorry. I did the only thing I could think of and ran away before I hurt someone for real."

"It's not always the greatest solution," I said. "But this time, it was probably for the best. We dealt with the imp problem."

"I feel like a freak, Uncle Chip. What do I do?"

I sat down on the bed beside her. "We'll start with some of the meditation exercises your aunt teaches you in between your weapons sessions. If you can calm your mind, you have a better chance of countering Gorrath's connection to you."

I leaned over and nudged her with my shoulder. "Maybe you can send some of your girl mojo back at him and make him crave a makeover."

A hint of a grin turned up the corners of her mouth. "Yeah, we could paint a lipstick face on that soccer ball, if we ever get it back."

"Aunt Rose is working on that. We'll ask her what our next steps are since things seem to be progressing faster now." I stood and returned to the door. "Get dressed. She'll be here soon, and she might have some other questions for you."

I pulled the door shut and leaned against the hallway wall for a second.

This wasn't just a small step forward in Gorrath's control—it was a giant, flaming leap. A damn portal to hell? That wasn't just influence, that was power. And Sadie did not know how to stop it.

We were running out of time. Fast.

15

Rose

I swerved the Firebird around a white-haired granny in a Toyota. She flipped me a one-fingered salute out the window, but I didn't care. The imp attack had me a little rattled. Things were moving faster than I liked with this whole Gorrath situation.

My phone rang, and I answered. "Hitch, what took you so long to call me back? You promised you wouldn't dodge my calls anymore."

"Do you know what time it is?"

"It's after ten. Wake up."

"Yeah, but it's a Saturday. I was in the middle of the most delicious dream."

I didn't want to hear the details. "Can it. There's a situation at the house. What do you know about sealing hell portals?"

"Uh, let me crack open my book of things they never teach you at mage school."

"So, nothing?" I asked.

"I know a little. You saying that demon ball opened up a portal *in the house?*"

"Yes. I don't know how exactly. I'm on my way there now. I'm swinging by your apartment. Be out front in five minutes, and I'll fill you in on what I know."

"Make it ten. I still have to pee."

"You have seven. Don't be late." I hung up and ran through my list of what needed doing this morning on top of the current emergency. I started another call.

"Yeah, Rose?" Warren said.

"How are you coming on tracking down those demon worshipers? We need to find that ball."

"It's not easy. The ownership of the temple land is set up through a series of shell corporations and off-shore entities. If it's owned by anyone around here, they're doing a good job of covering their tracks."

I didn't like the answer. I also would not get faster answers by yelling at my best investigator. "Fine, keep tracking. They're from around here somewhere, and they must have a place to go when they're not at the temple."

"For all I know, they hold their extra meetings in some guy's finished basement in the 'burbs. But I'll keep on the trail and hopefully something will come up. It would help if you could lend me some magical assistance. Can't Hitch help me out?"

"No, but Chip sent for someone who might be able to track the ball differently."

"Who does Chip know who can do that?"

"I'll tell you if it works out. I'm doubtful." I pulled the Firebird up to the curb downtown in front of where Hitch lived. "I gotta go. I'll check in this evening."

"Catch you later."

Hitch's apartment was upstairs above what was now a hairdresser. I stared at the stale sample images hanging in the front window and checked my watch. He had exactly two minutes before he was late.

I didn't like to be kept waiting and took some calming breaths to soothe my racing thoughts. Chip had been clear that the imps were taken care of and there was no current danger. I forced myself to accept that he knew what he was doing. It wasn't like when he first took guardianship of the kids years before. He'd gotten a certain level of experience around the Unusual world in which he lived.

A tap on the passenger window startled me from my thoughts. "Hey, Rose. Ya gonna let me in?"

I leaned over and unlocked the Firebird's passenger door and waited for Hitch to sit down. As soon as the door shut, I gunned the engine and took a sharp right turn at the next light.

Hitch let out a yelp while he tried to clip his seatbelt latch. "Easy does it. I can't help you if I'm dead."

"Don't be so sure. I know a really good necromancer."

Hitch closed his mouth and gripped the door handle so tightly his knuckles turned white. I smiled and sped up. We needed to get to the house.

Six minutes later, we pulled into Chip's neighborhood and stopped out front. I got out and grabbed my sword in its scabbard from behind the front seat. Hitch joined me as I jogged up to the front door. I had my key out and the door open in seconds, and we burst inside.

"Chip, where are you?"

"In the kitchen."

Hitch and I went through the house. The acrid brimstone smell irritated my sensitive Fae nose. There was also a hint of fresh coffee and a bit of wood smoke, too.

We entered the kitchen. Chip sat on a stool by the island, sipping from a mug of coffee.

He pointed at a line of five perfect imp statues lined up on the counter next to the stove. "See, I took care of it."

"What did you do?"

He reached out and hefted the cast iron frying pan in one hand. "This is now my favorite kitchen multi-tasker. It makes bacon and smacks down tiny demons, too."

Hitch smiled. "Cold iron. Good thinking. Be careful, though. They're not dead. Just awaiting reanimation."

That alarmed Chip, who'd clearly assumed the danger had passed. His discomfort gave me a little burst of pleasure after the way he had repeatedly assured me he had it all handled.

I glanced around the kitchen, taking in all the signs of the fight with the imps. "Where's the portal that opened?"

"Over there, underneath the overturned table."

"Chip, that's a portal to hell. You can't use a wooden table to block it off." I flipped the table and took a step back, my stomach twisting at what I saw.

The hole wasn't just a charred spot—it pulsed, like a wound in the fabric of reality. Inside, I caught flickers of movement: clawed hands grasping at the edges, distant howls rising up from the abyss.

A thin tendril of smoke curled out, smelling like burned flesh and sulfur.

I turned to Chip. "And you thought a wooden table would hold that?"

Chip's face paled. "I mean… It seemed sturdy at the time."

Hitch let out a low whistle. "That's… Uh. That's real bad. Yep. Very bad."

Chip came over to stand beside Hitch. "Can you close it?"

Hitch held a hand out over the opening and closed his eyes for a few seconds. He opened them and shook his head. "No, but I know someone who can."

"Good," I said. "Call them."

"Yeah, there's a problem there. I can't."

"Why not? Don't tell me you're holding out for more money?" I glared at him, preparing to let loose my full anger if he answered wrong.

"The person who might know how to close this is Gwinn." Hitch's face darkened. "I've been calling her and texting her for days, and she won't even answer me."

I crossed my arms. "Then we need another plan."

"No, no. It's not that." He let out a frustrated sigh and rubbed his temples. "It's just… She has a temper, okay? And when I say she's ignoring me, I mean she's blocking my number, cursing my house-plants, and sending very pointed hexes via email. If I ask her for a favor, she'll probably try to set my eyebrows on fire."

Chip raised a brow. "So… a normal breakup?"

"Shut up," Hitch and I said in unison.

I pulled the elastic band from my ponytail and shook out my long, black hair. Then I gathered it again while I thought about how I was going to handle this. I retied the ponytail and said, "Give me her number. I'll reach out to her."

"I don't think she's going to enjoy hearing from you, either. She knows you're a friend of mine."

"Let me handle that. In the meantime, you and Chip figure out a better way to block that hole that doesn't involve something flammable."

Hitch shrugged and held out his phone so I could see her contact information. I punched it into the messaging app and stepped back to compose my request. He was right. If the woman I last saw with my ex-boyfriend called me, I wouldn't answer her either.

Chip crouched down beside the hole in the floor. "We need to do something with this before more imps—or worse—find it."

"You got any sheet metal in the garage? We could nail it over the hole. It should hold temporarily."

"No." Chip stood and rubbed a hand across the back of his neck while he looked around. "The best I have that's the right size is the stainless-steel lid to my turkey fryer."

"Hmmm." Hitch leaned over the hole and used two hands to measure the opening. He pulled them back quickly and blew on them. "That is hot. Okay, get the lid. I have an idea. You have a cordless drill and some random screws, right?"

"I do. And I see where you're going. That's a good idea. I'll be right back." Chip ran over to the basement door and disappeared down the stairs.

By now, I had tried three different drafts of my text to Gwinn, and none of them looked right. I knew she was going to have a negative reaction to me.

Chip returned from his trip downstairs with a shiny steel lid about eighteen inches across. He also carried a cordless drill and a small tool-box. He handed the lid to Hitch, and the two of them crouched beside the portal.

I kept drafting the text message while they worked.

Five minutes and a lot of noise later, Chip stood up and nodded. "That is a perfect solution. Good thinking, Hitch."

They bumped fists bro-style.

I rolled my eyes and returned my attention to my phone. This wasn't going to work. If I were Hitch's ex, I'd want nothing to do with any of his friends, especially female ones. It was time to pivot in a direction I hated to go.

"Rose," Chip asked, "how's the message to the lady friend going?"

"I think we need to go with another plan." I steeled myself for the next part. "You need to be the one to reach out to her. Here's her number."

Chip shook his head. "She will not respond to a random text or call from some guy she doesn't know. Besides, I do my best work in person."

"That's what I'm afraid of," I said.

Chip frowned. "I didn't say I was going to date her. I was just going to turn on some of the classic Chip charm."

"Exactly. Just get her to commit to helping. That fryer lid isn't going to hold a determined demon back for long if they discover the opening." I pointed up. "Is Sadie in her room? I want to check on her."

Chip nodded. "She's upset about what happened. I told her it wasn't her fault, but… I don't know if she believes me."

I exhaled slowly. Sadie wasn't just upset. She was scared. And she had every right to be. This wasn't merely a fight—this was something growing inside her, something that could take everything she was and twist it into something else.

I tightened my grip on my sword. I'd spent my whole life fighting demons. But I'd never had to fight one inside someone I loved.

"I'll talk to her." I took a last glance at the portal, then turned to Chip. "You need to find Gwinn fast, but we also need another plan."

"What are you thinking?"

"Sadie can't keep fighting this alone. If Gorrath is growing stronger, we need to step up the search for someone who can sever his influence permanently."

"You mean a mage?" Hitch asked.

I shook my head. "No. I mean something stronger. A celestial warrior—an Eldara."

Chip's brows shot up. "You mean the Valkyrie?"

I nodded. "She might be the only one who can help Sadie before Gorrath takes full control. Find Gwinn first, then light a fire under Gibbie. We need the Eldara more than ever now. Hitch, you're on guard duty. Watch that hole and zap anything that tries to get through."

"I don't know what you think I can do if a major demon makes a play to enter this room, but I'll try."

I left Chip and Hitch to work out their tasks and headed upstairs to offer what I could to help Sadie deal with Gorrath.

16

Chip

I got little help from Hitch about Gwinn. Most of his comments amounted to variations on a "she's crazy" theme and that I'd better watch my back when dealing with her. I took it all in but didn't put much credence in it. Knowing Hitch for as long as I had, I didn't have much faith in his ability to judge others fairly. As far as I was concerned, Gwinn's desire to break up with Hitch was a check mark in the positive column.

The café where she worked was easy enough to find. She usually worked Saturday mornings, so she should be around until after the lunch rush. I figured I'd stop in and get a latte and a sandwich while I waited for her to get off work.

I walked inside and liked the vibe right away. A little bell on a spring over the door gave a pleasant jingle when I entered. A tall woman in her forties looked up from behind the counter and greeted me with a smile.

"Good afternoon, sir. I don't recognize you. Is this your first time visiting us?"

"As a matter of fact, it is. A friend recommended you, and I decided to come over and give it a try."

She pointed at the wall behind her. "There's the menu, and we have several off-menu specials, too, if you're adventurous. Our cook is always looking for a new favorite to add to the regular menu."

"Sounds good. Give me a second to choose something." I thought I knew what I wanted when I walked in, but the options on the menu for drinks and sandwiches opened up a host of other options. I stood there for a full minute while others entered and filtered past me before I made up my mind.

Decision made, I got in line behind the last person and waited my turn.

A shorter young lady with close-cropped dark hair stood behind the register. Her name tag read *Gwinn*.

"Hi, what can we get you?"

"I'd like a large hot peppermint latte with skim milk and a grilled cheese BLT. That sounds delicious."

"It's one of my personal favorites. You won't be disappointed. Will this be to go?"

"No, I thought I'd hang out and take in the vibe."

"Excellent. Grab a seat. I'll bring your drink and food out when they're ready. What's your name?"

"Chip." I leaned over the counter a little. "But you might want to know me as a guy with a little magic portal problem."

She quirked one eyebrow higher than the other, but that was the only reaction to my words. "Got it." She picked up a large coffee cup and a marker and wrote on the side of the cup. She turned and put it in line with the other cups waiting to be filled with their respective orders.

The small seating area had several open seats, and I picked a table in the corner where I could see both the front door and the counter. I leaned back against the wall and scrolled through my phone while I watched people come and go.

It took almost ten minutes before Gwinn walked around the counter with my latte and a white ceramic plate with my sandwich and chips.

"Here you go. I get off in an hour if you want to talk about that problem you're having." She set the plate and cup down and returned to her work.

I turned the latte cup around. Written on the side were the words "Portal Guy." I smiled. So far, things were going well enough. I started on the sandwich while it was hot. One bite in, and I leaned back and closed my eyes for a second. The taste explosion from the fresh tomatoes, along with the sharp cheddar and bacon, had my taste buds singing. I made a mental note to come back here soon. I'd bring the kids along, too. Both would enjoy the food and beverage choices.

My meal almost went down too fast. Even the homemade potato chips were worth savoring. I was in heaven.

I should have known it couldn't last.

The crowd had thinned out until I was alone in the café, aside from the two women behind the counter. A pair of women dressed all in black walked in. They went right up to the counter, and the taller one, with bright lavender hair, pointed at Gwinn.

"You are coming with us."

"I'm working, Geraldine. Tell the mistress I'll come by the coven house later if she wants to talk."

The short blonde crossed her arms. "You don't get to send an email announcing you're quitting the coven and expect to get away without consequences. Jessica wants to see you now."

"I said I'm working, Emi. Leave me alone."

The tall manager walked over. "How about I offer you ladies a drink on the house to enjoy while you wait? Gwinn's shift ends in a half hour."

"Stay out of this." Geraldine snapped her fingers and flicked her thumbnail off her teeth at the manager. The woman flew backward as if struck by a great force. She bounced off the counter, knocking over several bottles of flavored syrups, then slid unconscious to the floor.

"Hey, there was no cause for that." Gwinn wove her fingers in front of her in an intricate pattern and thrust her hands forward at Geraldine, thumbs touching and forefingers pointed at the target.

The spell washed over the tall witch, blowing her hair back as if in a stiff wind. Behind her, a table overturned, along with two chairs.

"You youngsters never learn." Geraldine shouted a pair of words and thrust her hands up at the ceiling.

I felt it before I saw it.

The air in the café turned thick, charged like the moment before a lightning strike. My shark's tooth charm went ice cold against my chest as a warning. I didn't need it—I could feel the weight of their magic pressing down like an unseen storm.

Then Gwinn hit the ceiling, and that was enough deciding for me. Time to move.

I stood and walked toward the pair of witches staring up at Gwinn.

"Ladies, ladies. Let's see if we can tone things down here for a moment. There's no need to tear up the whole place."

Behind the counter, the manager had regained consciousness. Fear kept her eyes wide as she nodded to agree with me. I smiled to reassure her. I was positive I could de-escalate this situation.

Emi turned a baleful glare in my direction. "We don't need the interference of any man in coven business. Leave or suffer the consequences."

"You may not want me to interfere, but if you keep using your magic openly this way, the local Unusual community will not be happy with you. I'll bet your Jessica won't be too pleased if you two bring down that kind of scrutiny on your coven."

Geraldine let go of her spell and faced me. Behind her, Gwinn crashed to the floor with a groan. "Since you don't heed our warnings, you are fair game in my book. I will enjoy turning you into a worm for a while. Hopefully, no one steps on you before the spell wears off."

She pointed a finger at me, and a ray of pale purple light shot out and splashed against my chest.

Nothing happened.

I smiled and raised a hand up while I formed a cylinder of force in my mind's eye. I snapped my fingers and dropped the curved Guardian barrier over the two witches.

Geraldine screamed and reached out to press her hands against the invisible shield. "What have you done? Where is this power coming from?"

"It's a little trick I picked up over the years. Maybe you won't run out of air before the magic wears off," I bluffed. I couldn't close off the top of the cylinders of force. There was plenty of air getting in there.

The witches didn't know that, though.

Emi said, "Perhaps we were hasty. We didn't intend to interrupt your meal. We only came for the girl."

"Unfortunately, she's coming with me. I have need of her services. Tell Jessica she's under my protection for the foreseeable future."

Geraldine's sinister glare indicated she wasn't ready to give up. "You won't get far. I suspect you can't carry our sister witch and maintain this barrier at the same time." She pounded a fist on the inside of the surrounding wall of force.

The impact of her blow resonated through me and sapped at the power I held. I had to draw on additional mana to hold up the shield. I kept up my facade of confidence, though.

"Gwinn, can you get up and come over here?"

Gwinn staggered slightly, rubbing her shoulder where she'd hit the floor. She shot me a sharp look, her expression torn between frustration and relief.

"What the hell did you just pull me into?"

I held up my hands. "Technically, I didn't do anything. You're the one quitting a coven."

Her lips pressed into a thin line. "Yeah, and normally that just gets you ghosted—not slammed into a ceiling." She sighed. "Fine. But if you get me killed, I swear I'll haunt your ass."

"I'm a friend of Hitch's. I have a problem, and he told me you could help me out. Come with me, take care of our portal issue, and we're square."

Geraldine growled, "If you go with him, it only delays the inevitable, sister. We will find you again and deal with your insolence."

That settled any reservations Gwinn had. "I don't have much choice. I guess I'm going with you."

"Good. Walk to the door and hold it open for me." I waited for her to start toward the entrance, then followed, keeping the force barrier in place around the two powerful witches.

Geraldine and Emi glared, pivoting to follow me out the door with their eyes.

I dug in my pocket with one hand, holding the other up to maintain my flowing magic. I found the SUV's key fob and gave it to Gwinn. "Go find my truck and bring it over here by the curb. I'll keep them in there until you get here, then we need to get out of here. I'm almost dry." My mana stores had run dangerously low. The witches inside pummeled my shield with their magic. The strength of their assaults resonated through my brain and gave me a pounding headache.

Gwinn wasn't gone long. She used the alarm on the key fob to locate the SUV and returned in under a minute. By that time, though, I was a quivering mess. Every muscle in my body felt like jelly as I drew every last ounce of energy to hold up the barrier inside the café.

The young witch leaned over to the passenger side and opened the door from the inside. "Come on. Let's go."

I pushed one last surge into the barrier and ran for the vehicle. As soon as I was inside and closing the door, Gwinn sped away.

As she hit the gas, I caught a glimpse of movement in the side mirror. Geraldine stood in the café doorway, watching us go. She didn't look mad. She looked... amused.

Geraldine raised a single finger to her lips, as if telling me to keep quiet about what had just happened.

Then the mirror cracked.

I swore and turned forward, heart hammering. This wasn't over. Not by a long shot.

Gwinn wove around the incoming cars entering the parking lot until we were out on Route 140 and putting plenty of distance between us and the vengeful witches we'd left behind.

"Where to?"

I pointed down the road. "Go this way for a while. I'll give you my address. That's where the portal is. Close it for me so I don't have to worry all that was for nothing. I don't like being on the wrong side of the local coven." I dug out my license and handed it to her.

"Portals are kind of my thing. Where's it go, anyway?" She took the license, glanced at the address, and set it down on the seat beside her.

"Hell."

"Oh, that should be fun. I've always wondered..."

I blinked hard. My hands were trembling on my knees, muscles weak, as if I'd just run ten miles with a cinderblock strapped to my chest.

The road blurred. I clenched my teeth, willing my focus to stay sharp, but the edges of my vision flickered with creeping black.

Gwinn said something else, but her voice stretched out, slow and distorted. My shark charm flared cold one last time before everything tilted sideways.

Then, nothing.

17

Rose

I heard the garage door going up from where I sat in the kitchen. Chip must be back with the witch. I sipped at my hot tea and checked the temporary patch on the portal with the toe of my boot to make sure it was still secure. I didn't trust the fryer lid to hold up long if something on the other side wanted to find a way through.

Rising, I set the mug down. Witches were always difficult to deal with. They had their own agendas around natural balance in the world that rarely matched up to the goals of those who fought for the greater good. I hoped Gwinn would not be a problem.

I opened the door to the garage. To my surprise, the girl was driving Chip's SUV. I checked the passenger seat through the windshield and saw him slumped down in the seat.

"What the hell did you do to him?"

Gwinn shut off the engine and closed the garage door before she got out. She held up a hand. "I didn't do anything. There was an altercation with a few members of my coven. This guy came to my rescue. He must've overused his magic because he passed out after he got in the truck."

I walked over and pulled open the passenger door. Chip flopped over and almost fell out. I had to act fast and push him back into the seat. He groaned and mumbled something.

"Chip, wake up. You're home."

Nothing but more groaned and incoherent words.

"Come help me get him inside."

Gwinn came over to stand beside me. "He looks heavy."

"He is. But we can't leave him out here. It's too cold. I can support him if you can help get him up in a fireman's carry on my shoulder."

Gwinn looked me up and down, as if sizing up my ability to handle the load.

"I'm way stronger than I look. Just help me."

Together, we pulled Chip over and across my shoulders. I resisted the urge to groan under his weight. I wouldn't give Gwinn the satisfaction at this point in my plan.

"Get the door."

Gwinn ran to open the door all the way and hold it for me while I took careful steps into the kitchen. I nodded at the door to the dining room and the rest of the house. "Get that one, too."

She moved around me and pushed open the swinging dining-room door.

I carried Chip through and over to the couch in the family room. He slid off onto the cushions, and I straightened up, stretching my back.

"I told you he was heavy."

"Hey, I got him in here, didn't I?" I walked back to the kitchen.

Gwinn followed me. "Is Hitch here? I really don't want to see him."

"No. He left to pick up some spell components he needs to track something down for me." I didn't want to share too much about our demon situation. It was always best to compartmentalize these things.

"The guy in there, Chip? He said you had a portal you needed help with. Something about an opening into hell?"

"Yes, it's over there in the corner by the table." I nudged the fryer lid with my boot, but even through the leather, I could feel the heat radiating up my shin.

Gwinn crouched beside it and frowned. "Yeah, this thing's a ticking time bomb."

A faint scratching noise drifted up from beneath the lid. My spine went rigid.

Gwinn tilted her head. "That… wasn't the house settling, was it?"

I didn't answer. I just reached for my sword.

"This is a clever solution. I don't think it'll last long before it sets the house on fire, though."

That alarmed me. I hadn't thought about that possibility. "It's that hot?"

Gwinn nodded and pointed at the mug of tea. "You have any more? I get thirsty when I'm working."

Putting the worry about the portal aside for a minute, I walked over and pressed the button on the handle of the electric kettle. The mugs were already right there next to it, hanging off pegs on the wall. I grabbed the box of tea from the cabinet and set it beside the kettle with the lid open. Chip had a nice selection of black, green, and herbal teas.

Gwinn joined me by the counter while we waited for the water to boil. She selected a minty green tea bag and grabbed a mug with wildflowers on it. "Once I handle the portal, I'll need a ride back to my car at the café."

"What was the deal with the witches Chip dealt with? Should we expect any blowback?" I knew Jessica, the current local coven leader. She was a stickler for the rules, and I didn't relish having a run-in with her over this.

"They found out I wanted out of the coven."

"You can't ever leave? What if you find a job in another city?"

"I want out. I don't want to move away. That's the problem. They don't like having women practicing natural magic in the area who aren't affiliated. They're very much a 'my way or the highway' kind of group."

I understood. Most of the covens I'd encountered were the same way about their members and anyone who encroached on their particular brand of magic. There were a few work-arounds, but the opportunities to take advantage of them were rare. One was patronage. In the old days, if you were a court mage or witch, you didn't have to belong to a coven. Your allegiance was to the throne.

That gave me an idea, but I needed to get to know Gwinn better first. If she were to associate with our family to avoid retaliation from the coven, I needed to know she'd be loyal as well as useful.

The water bubbled, and the kettle clicked to signify it was finished heating. I poured some water into Gwinn's mug. "Say when."

She watched the water level rise, nearing the rim, and nodded. "That's good. Thanks. Do you have sugar, or better yet, honey?"

"I think Chip has some honey in the pantry. Give me a sec." I went into the walk-in pantry and ducked down to peer into the back of each shelf until I found what I was looking for. I returned with a plastic bear squeeze container half full of honey.

"That's perfect. I recognize the label. It's from a local farm, which is even better." Gwinn drizzled some into her mug and stirred it with a spoon. She bobbed the tea bag at the end of its string a few times and then removed it, setting it on her spoon to keep it off the counter.

She picked up the steaming mug and sipped with her eyes closed. "That definitely hits the spot."

We sat on the stools by the counter in silence for almost ten minutes while Gwinn enjoyed her tea. I took advantage of the hot water and poured myself some English breakfast tea. I even added some honey and agreed with Gwinn that it was a perfect addition.

When she was almost finished with her tea, Gwinn set the mug down and said, "Okay, let's get to work on this portal problem you have. Care to tell me how you opened it? Did Chip do it by accident? I got the impression he wasn't completely comfortable with magic back at the café."

"No, we had a little wild magic leakage that opened up the portal. It's small, though."

Gwinn pointed at the five stone imps lined up along the wall. "Big enough for some baddies to get through."

"Yes, which is why we need to close it. Can you do it?"

"I think so. I will need a few things. They're pretty standard components. I would ordinarily ask Hitch to get them. Given our circumstances, though, I'd rather not."

"I understand. So does he, for that matter. He anticipated what you might need. He should be back soon with the stuff on his shopping list. If you'd rather not be around, I can meet him out front."

"No, I'm good." She chuckled to herself. "You probably think I was overreacting to what I thought was happening with you and him."

That got me laughing. "No, believe me, when I think of Hitch, I also expect the worst. It's not like he inspires confidence."

She laughed harder. "Right?"

"Exactly. Anyway, I don't judge people on their relationships." I thought back to my onetime dalliance with Chip. "We're all allowed to make a mess sometimes when it comes to personal relationships."

Gwinn lifted her mug toward me. "Amen, sister."

I clinked my mug against hers. "Amen indeed." She seemed competent. Practical. Maybe even trustworthy. But trust issues had gotten people killed before. I filed that thought away for later and took another sip of tea.

My phone buzzed. "Hey, that's Hitch. He's almost here." I glanced at Gwinn. "Last call on me letting him inside."

"Let him come. We're finished, and I need to get over him. Maybe some aversion therapy is in order."

"Given how angry I get at him sometimes, that might be good advice for me, too."

That drew a chuckle from us both again.

I texted Hitch to come to the garage door, and I got up to open it so he could come in. It was easier than walking all the way through to the front door. Addy was playing his Xbox in the media room upstairs, and Sadie was in her room, still upset over the earlier events of the day.

Hitch came in, chattering randomly as usual. "I had trouble finding the butterwort, but your man, Hitch, persevered. I found some seeds instead of the dried petals. Hopefully—" He stopped when he spotted Gwinn. "Oh, you're here already."

"Hello, Hitch."

"Um, yeah, hi." Hitch gave a half wave and quick-walked through the kitchen to set his worn leather shoulder bag down on the charred kitchen table.

I shot Gwinn a smile, and she returned it. We clearly both agreed he should be uncomfortable.

Gwinn said, "Did you remember to get the bat wing and sulfur powder?"

"Of course." Hitch's sudden defiant tone disappeared as fast as it had shown itself. He nodded an apology before digging in the bag and setting the ingredients out on the table.

Gwinn inspected the spell components, frowning. "At least you didn't forget anything."

Hitch scoffed, crossing his arms. "Give me some credit. I even got the good sulfur powder—not the cheap synthetic stuff."

She blinked. "Wait, really?"

He smirked. "What can I say? I know a guy."

She narrowed her eyes like she wanted to argue, but I caught the flicker of reluctant approval in her expression before she turned away.

"Well, for once I won't have to send you back out for something you forgot."

Hitch twitched his mouth like he wanted to say something, then changed his mind. That was probably wise.

The kitchen door opened, and Chip stumbled in, rubbing at his temples with two fingers of each hand. His usually tanned skin looked pallid under the kitchen light, and there were dark circles under his eyes.

"Oh, my God," he groaned. "I have the worst headache in history."

I moved toward him instinctively before I caught myself. Instead, I leaned back against the counter and crossed my arms. "Serves you right. Gwinn said you nearly ran yourself dry back at the café."

"Remind me never to do that again."

His voice wavered slightly. That was enough for me—I stepped forward, ready to catch him if he fell. He steadied himself against the counter and forced a weak smile.

Gwinn huffed. "Men. Always overextending yourselves and acting surprised when it bites you in the ass." She got up, grabbing a small bit of the birch bark powder from the table. "Here, I'll steep you a tea that'll fix up that headache in no time."

"Really?" Chip asked. His bleary eyes pled for some help. "You sure it's no trouble?"

"Not at all. Sit on the stool." She picked through the tea box until she found a selection she liked and dropped the tea bag in an empty mug from the wall rack. Then she held the pinch of birch bark over the mug and rubbed her thumb and forefinger together to sprinkle the powder in beside the tea bag.

It didn't take long to heat the water again. As soon as it boiled, she poured enough to fill half the mug. Gwinn stirred the mixture. "Hitch, get me a couple of ice cubes from the freezer."

"On it." Hitch pulled open the freezer door. He fished out a couple of oblong ice cubes from the automatic ice maker box inside.

"Put them in the tea. It's too hot to drink, and he needs to down it quickly for the magic to work."

Hitch dropped the ice into the mug. Gwinn clapped her hands together over the mug and muttered something under her breath. The contents of the mug glowed a golden hue for a few seconds before it faded.

She handed the mug to Chip. "Here. The ice has cooled it. Drink it all while it's still warm."

Chip took the mug and stared inside for a second, then took a deep breath and drained the tea in one go.

He set the mug down and steadied himself against the counter with his free hand. "Ugh, that's horrible." He pointed at the bottle of honey. "Couldn't you have added that?"

"Of course, but medicine is supposed to taste bad. That's how you know it's working." She looked my way and winked.

I hid a grin behind my hand. I think I liked this young witch.

Chip blinked a few seconds later and sat up straight. "Hey, I think it worked."

"Of course it worked," Gwinn said. "You think I'm a hack?"

"No, no, that's not what I meant at all. I was just surprised. I've never had a headache go away so quickly before."

She shrugged. "It helped that it was magical in nature. Potions always heal magical ailments faster." She walked back over to the table and put her hands on her hips. "Okay. I think it's time to address this portal problem you have."

18

Chip

With my headache taken care of, I was ready to help out. "What do you need to close the portal?"

Gwinn looked around the kitchen. "I don't suppose you have a cauldron?"

"Uh, no. I have a big pot for steaming crabs. It's not cast iron. I think it's aluminum."

"That'll do in a pinch." Gwinn walked over to where Hitch had laid out the ingredients. "Fill it about a quarter full of warm tap water and set it down over here."

I reached up to the cabinet over the refrigerator and pulled down the big aluminum crab pot, which had a steamer basket inside. I pulled that out and handed the empty pot and lid to Gwinn.

She filled it in the sink and carried it over to the kitchen table. After setting it down, she stared at the multiple ingredients spread across the table in containers and packets.

"This is going to come together fast once I get going. Before I start, we'll need a paintbrush—like you'd use on the walls, not for artwork. You'll need to be ready to unscrew the lid from atop the portal when I give the order. Then everyone has to follow my commands to the letter.

Most portals close on their own. This one is persistent and is going to require special measures."

We all nodded. I held up the cordless drill with the screwdriver bit, ready to go. Rose stepped close, holding the scabbarded sword at her side in her left hand. Hitch stood ready beside the table with Gwinn.

"Good," Gwinn said. "Hitch, hand me the ingredients when I ask for them. Have all the containers or paper packets opened."

The mage prepared the ingredients that needed opening and then nodded.

Gwinn took a deep breath, blew it out, and leaned over the makeshift cauldron. She held out her hand. "Sulfur powder."

Hitch handed over the ingredients one at a time as she asked for them. The witch added them in varying amounts to the crab pot. She didn't seem to measure but was very exact, sometimes adding a partial pinch of a powder to what she'd already added or breaking a large piece into a few smaller pieces before selecting one to put in.

To my amazement, steam started rising from the pot despite there being no source of heat. A subtle white glow lit the rising steam from below, too.

Gwinn held her hands over the pot and chanted in a choppy, guttural language. The glow grew brighter, and the steam got thicker, rising from the bubbling material inside.

I was gripping the drill's handle so hard my fingers ached. I passed the tool to my left hand and flexed my stiff fingers a few times. Now wasn't the time to tense up.

The process continued with alternating bouts of chanting and the addition of more of the ingredients until a pungent odor had filled the entire kitchen. It smelled sort of like the stinky love child of rotten eggs and sweaty underwear.

"We're ready to go," Gwinn said finally. "Open the cover on the portal. Hitch, get the brush ready. When I tell you, paint the mixture around the opening in a broad circle, then fill in the center until you paint the actual portal itself."

"Got it." Hitch held up the paint brush.

I knelt down and began loosening the screws we'd drilled through the steel lid. The heat rising from it made beads of sweat pop up on my forehead. Some of them dropped to sizzle on the surface of the heated lid.

I removed the last screw and stood. "It's ready to move."

Rose had retrieved an oven mitt from beside the stove. She bent down and looked up at Gwinn.

"Do it. Hitch, start painting as soon as she moves out of the way."

Rose lifted the lid by its handle and stepped back. Hitch crouched and started painting a circle, using the brownish paste from the crab pot Gwinn held for him. He started a few inches away from the hole and left a space of charred floorboards between the circle and the round opening.

I leaned over. Something didn't look right. "Hey, I can't see all the way down to the lava rivers anymore. Something is covering the portal on the far side."

Hitch stopped painting after finishing the initial circle. "You could see all the way down?"

"Yeah. That piece of leathery material wasn't there before."

The portal pulsed with a sickly red glow. Heat rippled through the air, thick and humid, carrying the scent of scorched stone and decay.

A low murmur drifted up from the depths, a chorus of distant, distorted voices—whispering in a language that made my skin crawl.

They knew our names.

Then, without warning, the leathery surface shifted. A bloodshot eye snapped open, unblinking, its reptilian pupil filling the opening— focused directly on me.

Hitch yelped and leaped backward.

The eye fell away from the opening, exposing more of the leathery hide all around it. A thick tentacle thrust up through the portal, its end covered with both suckers and spiky pinions. It wrapped around Hitch's leg from his ankle up to his thigh.

"Yow! It's got me!"

I stomped my foot on the four-inch-thick tentacle. When nothing happened, I lifted my foot and rammed it down again, grinding my heel into the leathery, spike-covered flesh.

A second tentacle snaked up through the portal and reached for me. I leaped back, slamming into the wall close behind me. There was nowhere to go to escape the creature.

The new tentacle coiled around both my knees. I gritted my teeth as its spiked suckers dug into my legs. Every movement sent jolts of pain up my thighs. I yanked at the slick, oozing flesh, but the hooked barbs refused to let go.

Beside me, Hitch let out a strangled gasp. His fingers clawed at the limb around his ankle, his face contorted in pain. "It's crushing my leg," he choked out, eyes wide with panic.

Rose swung her blade with a blur of blue fire. The Fae steel struck the thickest part of the tentacle—but instead of cleaving straight through, it lodged halfway in. A grotesque shriek erupted from the portal, and the tentacle convulsed, tightening instead of letting go.

With a guttural snarl, Rose twisted the sword, wrenching it free and hacking again. This time, the blade sliced cleanly, black ichor spraying across the floor as the severed limb spasmed violently.

The remains of the tentacle around my legs twitched but didn't let go. I reached down to unwrap it while Rose helped extricate Hitch from the other demonic member.

Gwinn hadn't even flinched when the tentacles burst from the portal. Now, she muttered a sharp incantation and slammed her palm against the side of the crab pot.

A pulse of blue energy surged through the mixture, thickening the steam into an opaque mist. "That should buy you a few seconds," she called out. "Finish painting the mixture around the portal. Rose, keep the creature on the other side at bay any way you can. This spell's power is waning fast."

The stumps of the severed tentacles receded to be replaced by three more, filling the entire portal with their writhing, twisting limbs.

I grabbed the oozing remnant wrapped around my knees and tugged on it. The spiky hooks tore at my skin and blue jeans, and I gritted my teeth at the pain. With a grunt, I jerked the remnant free and tossed it in the corner. I reached back with my right hand and pulled the hilt from its clip on my belt. A quick, directed thought extended the blade to its full length.

It was just in time.

One of the three tentacles swung in my direction, its hooks scratching my arm. I yanked my hand back to avoid its grip.

The writhing arm reached for me again, but I hacked down with the Guardian sword and sliced a sliver from it.

Black blood sprayed from the open wound, slickening the wrappings on my sword's hilt.

I tightened my grip and readied for another strike. Now wasn't the time to lose my weapon. I reversed my swing and caught the tentacle with a glancing backhanded blow, the flat of the blade swatting it away from me.

Next to me, Rose twisted and danced, dodging two of the reaching tentacles at once while she sliced and slashed at them.

Hitch crawled forward on the floor, his leg trailing blood. He slid the aluminum pot next to him and reached forward to continue painting the thickening paste around the opening.

"Hurry, the spell is almost spent," Gwinn said. "You must clear the opening before he finishes painting over it."

Rose shouted her war cry in the old high Fae language and charged forward. Her blade wove a blurred, spinning circle of death in front of her.

I knew she'd take care of the two tentacles facing her. I had to deal with the one menacing me.

The tentacle pulled back from me, and I let my guard down. But it was only winding up for its next attack.

The sudden swing of the thick tentacle splatted me against the wall like I was an annoying little fly. The air whooshed from my lungs.

I slumped to the floor, coughing to catch my breath. My sword skittered across the hardwood.

The tentacle raised up over me, and I took the only action I could. I drew upon my severely limited mana reserves for a single, focused dart of my force wall.

The cone-shaped magical projectile struck the tentacle where it emerged from the floor. I guided its needle-like tip as it drove into the fleshy stump. A gaping hole appeared. The tentacle spasmed twice, then flopped to the floor.

I scrambled on all fours over to where my sword lay and hacked at the limp arm until I'd severed it completely. Rose had dispatched the other two, leaving three twitching stumps protruding from the floor.

Hitch had painted the rest of the floor inside the initial circle around the portal.

Gwinn shouted, "Clear the opening and paint over it to seal the gap."

Rose didn't hesitate. She stomped down with her booted heel again and again on the stump ends. She drove them downward until they slipped from the hole, exposing the opening into the netherworld.

I saw more tentacles writhing below and called out to Hitch. "Quick, paint it shut. There's more down there ready to attack."

On his hands and knees, Hitch dipped the brush into the pot and slapped a thick line of the magical paste down next to the hole. He used the bristles to drag the mixture across the opening, where it hung in space as if painted on glass.

Hitch frantically continued until he'd covered the entire portal. He leaned back, upright on his knees, while we all stared at the former opening to hell.

I gripped my sword and waited for something to surge up through the painted opening. When nothing happened for several seconds, I dared to relax.

"Gwinn, that's it? It's really sealed?" I asked.

She nodded. "It worked. I can no longer feel the sinister forces trapped on the other side." The young witch reached out with one hand and helped Hitch to his feet. "Let me know if you want help with the other portal in town."

I did a double take. "What other portal?"

"The one at the high school. That was the first one I sensed. I was curious and went to investigate it. It's partially sealed already from the inside, but it's still there."

Rose caught my eye, and I nodded. It must be how Gorrath had come through.

"We need to check that out," I said. "It might be how he's channeling his power and maintaining the link to Sadie."

"I agree," Rose said. "Let's clean up here. We'll head over to the high school once that's done."

I retracted my sword blade into the hilt and clipped it back onto my belt. Then I joined the others as we gathered up the pieces of demon tentacles from the floor. A few of the larger ones still twitched from time to time. That creeped me out, but I kept working.

Soon we had it all bagged up and in the trash cans out front. We included the stone imp statues. As I closed the lid, I wondered if the folks at the landfill outside of town considered demon parts a hazardous material.

I shrugged. What they didn't know wouldn't hurt them.

19

Rose

Gwinn came with me on the trip to the high school. I figured she didn't want to ride in the same vehicle with Hitch if she didn't have to. Chip followed in the SUV, with Hitch riding shotgun and the kids in the back. We didn't dare leave Sadie home by herself with Gorrath still out there.

"So, what's the deal with you and Chip?" Gwinn asked.

Her offhand tone was almost too matter-of-fact. She probably wanted to know if he was available. It irked me how well the Chip charm worked regardless of the situation.

"We work together to raise the kids, but we're not together that way, if that's what you're asking."

"Oh, no. I was just wondering." She looked out the Firebird's passenger window for a second before asking, "What's he do for a living?"

"He's a stay-at-home uncle. We decided it was important for him to give up his work when he became the kids' legal parent."

"Oh, that's nice." More silence.

"Look," I said. "I won't get in your way if you want to date Chip. The only thing I'll say is it's a buyer beware situation."

She studied my face while I drove. After a bit, she said, "I appreciate the advice. I was just curious, that's all."

We arrived at the school, and I drove around the rear of the main building to where the athletic fields were located. I parked next to the main stadium entrance and got out. It was dark, and the field's lights were off since there was no game or practice. That was good. We wouldn't draw any attention while we were here.

I grabbed my sword from behind the seat and walked over to where Chip had pulled in a few parking spaces away.

He'd gotten out and popped the rear liftgate. He raised the floor panel in the back, revealing a small collection of bladed weapons. "Kids, grab your weapons. I don't expect you'll have to defend yourselves, but better safe than sorry."

"Awesome," Addy exclaimed. "Dibs on the axe." He grabbed a short-hafted battle axe with a double head and a short spike jutting up from between the two blades.

Sadie reached around her brother and selected a cross-hilted blade I recognized as her personal custom longsword. I was surprised Chip had let her bring it.

"Expecting trouble?" I asked.

"You've got your sword, too. I want the kids to be able to defend themselves if we run into more demons here."

"Fair enough. Let's see about this portal." I waved Gwinn over. "Can you lead us to it?"

"Sure. It's in the middle of the playing field." The witch entered where the sidewalk passed through a gap in the fence beside the field house and concession stand.

Hitch followed, with me close behind. Chip and the kids brought up the rear.

Gwinn led us out to the place where Sadie had collided with the other player during the game and we had first discovered the game ball was affected. "This is it. It's been partially sealed. See?" She stomped her foot on the grass. "Something pulled the firmament of our reality over the opening."

I knelt down to inspect the area around where Gwinn stood. My Fae senses tuned into the magical spectrum, and I saw what the witch meant. There was an arcane gap there, visible beneath the sod. It was more of a jagged tear than the perfectly circular portal created back at the house. Along the edges of the tear, a pulsing red glow showed an active spell in place to hold the portal in its current state.

I stood. "This is being maintained. That means someone or something would have to come back here and replenish the mana feeding the spell."

"You are correct." The man's voice wasn't Chip's.

A ripple of cold crawled up my spine. I turned my head slowly. Two figures stood halfway between us and the grandstands. They hadn't been there a moment ago.

My sword was in my hand before I'd even thought about it. "Chip—"

"I see them." His Guardian blade hissed as it extended.

The taller of the two figures shifted, his long, stringy blond hair barely masking his glowing yellow eyes. The other, a hunched old man, tilted his head at an unnatural angle. Even without using my Fae sight, I could sense the weight of their demonic forms pressing against reality.

The old man smiled. "You need not draw your weapons. We come to talk."

"Uncle Chip," Sadie said. "Those—"

Chip nodded. "—Are the demon men from the supermarket."

"What do you want?" I asked. "If you wish to return home via this portal before we seal it, you may pass peacefully. We will not harm you."

The younger demon said, "You must not seal the portal before Gorrath is captured."

The older one held up his hand to stop the other. "Our leaders sent us to retrieve Gorrath and bring him to justice in our realm. He was in the middle of his trial when this opening ripped open our court's roof and sucked him away."

Chip took a step forward, coming to my side. "What are you, the demon police?"

"Our name is not pronounceable in your tongue, but the meaning is similar. We have been given a task and may not return until it is accomplished or we are destroyed."

I lowered my sword, keeping it ready alongside my leg. "You're in no condition to take on the human cult that has Gorrath. Both of you are wounded."

"We didn't consider the natural weaknesses of these forms when we assumed them. It has been many years since our kind walked among the humans."

The younger one said, "None of that matters. We have been given our charge, and we must complete the task set before us. Our injuries will not stop us."

"Why not return to your plane and let us close the rift between our worlds?" Gwinn asked. "We will take care of the other demon for you. This portal is creating instability that will affect many in the area if it isn't dealt with."

"Only one from the outer planes can defeat Gorrath," the old demon said. "He is one of the Old Ones of our kind."

I nodded. "Gorrath is a demon lord. Killing him would require a special weapon wielded by one of the heavenly warriors, or a netherworlder, such as yourselves."

"So, you understand why you must let us complete our task?"

"Heavenly warrior?" Chip said. "If you mean one of the Eldara, then we're good. Gibbie said he was on it."

"Your cousin actually knows the Valkyrie rumored to hang around Elk City?" I never expected that avenue to work out.

Chip pulled out his phone. His thumbs worked on the screen as he tapped something into it. "Gibbie said he would take care of it. That was yesterday. He's never failed us before. I assume that meant he knew this Eldara warrior."

The two demons exchanged a glance, then the older one spoke. "One such as you describe would be helpful in apprehending Gorrath, but he is powerful. You will need our assistance. We may not return without him, and we cannot let you seal the rift."

I didn't like this. Keeping a portal to the netherworld open was insane. We should seal it now and be done with it.

But if these two were telling the truth, Gorrath was far beyond our ability to handle alone.

I stole a glance at Sadie. Her hands were clenched into fists, the blue glow of her Fae magic pulsing faintly around her fingertips.

If we lost control of Gorrath, she would be his first target.

I exhaled. "Very well. We agree to hold off on closing the rift… for now. However, you will obey us and follow our lead when it comes to tracking down and dealing with Gorrath." I didn't want anything happening to him until we could sever the connection to Sadie. I had no way to know what would occur if we destroyed the demon-possessed ball before that.

The two turned their heads and spoke back and forth in low voices. I only knew bits and pieces of the demon language, but part of the guttural exchange in the demon tongue sounded familiar. It sounded like "we cannot trust them."

I nodded. The feeling was mutual.

After their exchange ended, the old demon said, "We agree to your terms. For the time being, our goals are the same."

I noted the qualifier in the statement of allegiance. They'd stay with us only as long as our needs matched theirs.

"Where are you staying?" I asked. "We'll need to be able to contact you when the Valkyrie arrives."

The older demon gestured back at the grandstand. "We have been abiding beneath this structure using cloaking magic to conceal ourselves. We are concerned about the large numbers of humans who gather here. The proximity of so many could cause the rift to widen by accident. Our magic has been stabilizing the opening and keeps it from growing in size. Such an occurrence would be detrimental to both our worlds."

Sadie frowned. "So, um… if a bunch of people walk over this thing, it might pop open?"

Before anyone could answer, the ground shuddered beneath us— just for a second. A faint, sulfurous smell curled into the night air.

Gwinn's lips pressed into a tight line. "Yeah. That's not a theory. That's a certainty."

"Sadie," I asked. "When's the next soccer game here?"

"Monday night. They rescheduled the Liberty match. I hoped I'd be able to play."

I pointed down at the rift. "Will it hold while you accompany us to apprehend Gorrath?"

"I believe so," the younger demon said. "I was tasked with completing the spell. It is as strong as I can make it."

Gwinn said, "Is there anything we can do to bolster it? I could try to add reinforcement to it."

The old one shook his head. "No, your magic is not compatible with ours. You draw on this world, while ours is connected to the power of the lower planes."

She shrugged. "It was worth a try."

"Okay," I said. "We need everyone here to complete what needs to be done. Gwinn, you'll be responsible for closing this portal completely when the demons are finished and have passed through to their side. Hitch can help you. Chip will make sure his cousin comes through with our Eldara." I turned back to the demons and tapped my chest. "I am called Rose. You are?"

The older demon said, "I have been called Azith when named by humans. My companion is known as Dezik."

"Very well. Our next step is to locate Gorrath and the cult that is protecting him."

"We can assist with that," Dezik said. "I am a tracker. I have sensed Gorrath to the west of this city. We were formulating a plan to take him when you arrived."

"Good. Come with us, and we will pinpoint the location on a map so we can devise a course of action once the Eldara arrives."

Azith nodded. "We will follow your lead for the time being."

Chip moved close and whispered, "Do you think it's a good idea to invite them into the house?"

"In this case, we're better off knowing exactly where they are. Keeping them close is the best course of action. We can't let them take Gorrath without severing the tie to Sadie."

Chip shrugged. "It's as good a plan as any other, I guess." He raised his voice. "Let's load back up and head home. You two kids ride back with your aunt and Gwinn. I'll take Azith and Dezik with me and Hitch in the SUV."

He led the way while I waited to bring up the rear. As I turned to follow Chip, a cold prickle ran down my spine.

Azith and Dezik fell into step behind us, but the way Azith's gaze lingered on Sadie just a second too long sent a warning bell ringing in my skull.

The enemy of my enemy was an ally. For now.

I just hoped we weren't making a deal with something worse than Gorrath.

20

Chip

It was late when we headed back to the house after our trip to the second portal. Gwinn claimed the front passenger seat, which put Hitch in the back with the two demons. To say the vibe was odd inside the SUV was an understatement.

Hitch crossed his arms and stared out the window, doing a good impression of a kid in time-out. Dezik kept tapping a claw-like fingernail against the leather seat. Just awkward tension, thick as swamp air.

No one spoke for the fifteen-minute trip home.

As I drove to the end of the street where our house was located, my headlights lit a beat-up white Chevy van that was parked out front. I thought I recognized it and smiled.

I pulled into the driveway and clicked the button to raise the garage door. Two figures exited the van and walked across the yard in our direction while Rose parked in the driveway.

I climbed out and walked around the rear of the SUV, my grin broadening. "Gibbie. It's good to see you."

Sadie and Addy spotted their distant cousin too. "Cousin Gibbie!" They both ran over to the slightly overweight vampire and latched on with their hugs.

Gibbie returned the hugs, laughing at the welcome from his family, and when Addy stepped back, he tousled the boy's hair. "Hey, you guys. You're both getting so big."

I walked over and shook my cousin's hand. "It's good to see you. I hoped you'd be able to help us."

"I'm always available for family, Chip. I was happy to come help."

A striking, dark-haired woman, a little taller than Gibbie, walked around from behind him. She wore black jeans, high-heeled leather boots, and a leather jacket. Her confident stride, all sharp lines and battle-readiness, told me we'd found our Valkyrie.

I nodded toward her. "This the Valkyrie you mentioned?"

"Yes." Gibbie gave a big grin. "This is Ingrid, a Valkyrie and a good friend."

The woman gave a quick nod. "Gibson said you had a demon problem?" Her crisp British accent was a pleasant surprise.

"We do." I was going to say more but was interrupted by a bright, incandescent silver blade appearing in Ingrid's hand.

She crouched, ready to spring forward.

Azith and Dezik had gotten out of the SUV and moved up behind me.

"Hey, easy." I held out my hands and stepped between the woman and the two demons. "They're with us."

"You sent for me to come kill demons. Now I'm asked to stop. I'm confused." Ingrid rounded on Gibbie. "Did you lie to me?"

Gibbie took a step back. "No, I swear. There's got to be an explanation. Chip, can you tell her?"

"They're demon police. They're here to apprehend the same demon we need you to help hunt down."

Ingrid straightened from her battle crouch. "Demon police? There is no such thing. They've lied to you."

"No, Eldara, we have not lied." Azith took a step up beside me. "This human's explanation is simplistic, but not entirely untrue. A demon court has dispatched us to return Gorrath for his sentencing."

"And it is this Gorrath that we are after?"

"Yes," I said. The light of Ingrid's celestial blade lit up the entire front yard. "Let's take this inside before the neighbors start asking questions."

Ingrid lowered her sword, and the intensity of its light diminished to a soft glow at her side. She didn't return it to its scabbard—or wherever she'd retrieved it from.

I led the way inside, followed by Azith and Dezik. Rose brought up the rear. We passed through the kitchen, and I took everyone into the combination dining room and family room.

"Let's get settled here, and we can talk about our next steps," I said. "Addy, you and Sadie go up and get ready for bed. It's late."

Sadie shook her head. "This has to do with me. I have that demon in my head. It's my right to stay up for any discussion you have about it."

I considered her words. She stood straight and confident, and I glimpsed the queen she was to become in her stance. "Very well. Addy, you go upstairs. Sadie, you can stay."

Addy stomped a foot. "That's not fair."

"I didn't say it was, but that's what we're doing." I stared him down. "Go, Addy. I'll be up in a bit, and I'll let you know what we discussed if you're still up."

Addy's shoulders slumped. He slowly climbed the stairs up to his room.

"Uh, Ingrid. We're safe here in our home. Do you mind?" I nodded at the blade she still carried.

The Valkyrie flicked her wrist, and the sword was gone. I didn't see where it went. One second it was there. The next it wasn't.

"You mentioned Gorrath was our target. Is that the same Gorrath who led the attack on the steppes of Russia over a millennium ago?"

Azith nodded. "Yes, it is. You were there?"

"My sisters and I were present to collect the souls of valiant warriors who died in the fight against evil. We were there for the fight, as well. We accounted for our share of demon kills that day."

Rose said, "That was one of the last battles against the demon hordes and their earthly allies, wasn't it?"

Ingrid moved to the upholstered chair beside the sofa and sat down. "It was the turning point in the long campaign over the fate of the earth. Everything after that defeat was foreordained. We just had to complete the tasks laid out before us."

Azith stood opposite Ingrid, taking a place beside the fireplace with Dezik beside him. The older demon said, "We saw the error of our misguided efforts to overcome this place. Victory was not to be ours. Many returned to the nether planes, and we began many centuries of infighting and conflict amongst ourselves."

"And Gorrath has returned to the earth now?" Ingrid asked. "What is his purpose in coming here at this time?"

"It was an accident, we think." I explained the incident from the soccer game with no details about how Sadie's strong ties to wild magic had likely been responsible for opening the rift that allowed Gorrath to slip through.

When I got to the part about the soccer ball, Ingrid let out a barking laugh. "The demon lord is trapped inside a child's toy?"

"He is not without power or resources," Rose said. "There is still a tie to my niece, and he has found allies within a cabal of demon worshipers here in the community."

Ingrid studied Sadie for a second. "What is the tie to the girl? I don't see any demonic presence or possession."

Sadie answered before I could step in. "It's like he magnifies my negative emotions. I get angry much easier, and sometimes power just sort of leaks out of me. I try to keep control, but with him in my head, it sometimes gets away from me."

Ingrid pressed her lips in a firm line. "I sense a resolute strength in you, girl. You must resist his inclinations. Use that power within you to press back. Try now."

"What do you mean?"

"Find that place deep inside your mind where Gorrath lurks and press on it hard. It is your place, not his. Do not let him dictate what happens to you."

I looked to Rose for a sign if I should stop this or let it continue. Eldara were representatives of the powers of light, but that didn't mean they couldn't have their own motives with little regard for the life of one young Fae girl.

Every instinct screamed at me to pull Sadie back, protect her. But she was already too far into the fight. And, deep down, I knew this was her battle, not mine. Still, it tore at me. She was just a kid. My kid. My heart thundered against my ribs like it was trying to break free and protect her itself.

Rose met my eyes and gave a quick nod to let me know she thought this was okay.

Sadie closed her eyes and stood still behind the couch with her hands at her sides. After a few seconds, she squeezed them tighter until the skin crinkled at the corners of her eyelids. "I. Found. Him."

"Good," Ingrid said, her voice soft and encouraging. "Focus your will, and when you're ready, release it all in a single point on that presence in your mind."

Sadie kept her eyes closed and shook her head. "What if he fights back?"

"He almost certainly will. You're the person who anchors him to this place. If the connection to you is severed, he becomes much more vulnerable. Focus. Do it. Now."

Sadie's hands clenched into fists, and her entire body quivered.

Ingrid kept talking, never taking her eyes off my niece. "Press as hard as you can. Try to squeeze him out of existence. He's a bug. Crush him beneath your will."

Sadie's breath hitched. "He... grinning at me." Her voice dropped an octave, eerie and otherworldly. "He thinks this is funny."

"Ignore him," Ingrid snapped. "Press. Now."

Sadie's head whipped back and forth, her body rigid. "He won't let go."

"That demon isn't in charge. You are. It's your mind. He's like any other adult trying to tell you what to do. Refuse him. Send him away."

Sadie's head stopped moving, and she locked her face forward. Her eyebrows scrunched down above her eyes, and her lips curled up in a snarl of rage. She let out a roar that shook the room, raw power crackling in the air like a lightning storm with nowhere to strike.

Ingrid got up and stood next to Sadie. "Yes. Send him on his way. You have him. Don't give up."

The roar of power increased in volume until the crystal in the chandelier rattled.

Then there was nothing.

Sadie's knees sagged.

Ingrid was there and reached out to lend her support. She walked the girl around to the front of the couch and lowered her down to lean back on the cushions.

Sadie's eyes fluttered open, and I realized I had been holding my breath. I let it out with a long sigh. She was okay.

"He's gone. He really is."

Ingrid crouched in front of her. "You were marvelous. You will grow to be a strong woman indeed, Sadie. Your family should be proud."

The Valkyrie stood. "That is done. Now we have a way to track the demon lord. I was able to follow back as his awareness left Sadie's mind."

Rose stood. "Wait, you did all that just so you could track Gorrath? It had nothing to do with helping my niece?"

"The most important thing was to get him to come to the surface and fight back. I had to use her to do that. It was necessary, and now we have him."

This was exactly what I had been afraid of.

Rose realized her mistake in letting it proceed. "We had other ways of tracking him." Rose pointed at Azith and Dezik. "They could have led us to him."

"I could not afford to risk their loyalty to this cause. Demons have their own agendas."

Rose stalked over to Ingrid and stood nose to nose with her. "So do the Eldara, it seems. You had no right to endanger her if you weren't doing this for her benefit."

"What are you angry about? It worked. The girl is free of the demon now."

Rose's hand dropped to her side, and for a second, I thought she was going to draw the sword at her side.

I stepped over and gently inserted myself between the two, forcing each to take a step back. "Hey, I'm not a fan of the way this happened, either. But it's over, and we've had a positive outcome for all concerned. Let's focus on that."

"I'm not sorry we did it," Sadie said. "I hated having him there in the back of my mind. He whispered lies, trying to twist my thoughts, make me someone I'm not. He's gone, and I'm glad of it."

"I meant what I said. You are a remarkable young woman of great strength. Your power will rival my own someday, and yet, that thought doesn't give me concern. You will be a force for good." Ingrid walked across the room to the liquor cabinet on the hutch by the dining room table. "Let's see if you have anything decent in here."

"Try the single malt Scotch in the black bottle." I walked over to join her. "I think a toast is in order now that my niece is safe, one way or another."

Ingrid removed the bottle I'd indicated and twisted the cork free. I lined up five glasses for the non-demons present. Ingrid poured a few fingers of the amber liquid in each, and I handed them out to Rose, Gwinn, and Hitch. I picked up one of the remaining pair, and Ingrid lifted the other. Sadie came over and stood with her hands in her pockets.

"Sorry, kiddo. None for you just yet." I smiled when she returned my grin.

Ingrid lifted her glass. "To the beginning of a great defeat of the demon lord Gorrath."

We all raised ours, too.

Ingrid drained her glass. "Now, the hunt begins."

I clinked my glass against Rose's, then looked over at Sadie—finally free, but still a little pale.

One battle was over. But the war? It was coming.

21

Rose

We finished the toast, and Chip left to clean up the glasses in the kitchen. My phone buzzed. It was Warren. I scanned the message, and my breath caught. He'd found something. Maybe *the* thing.

"Chip," I called. "I'm heading out. Warren might have Gorrath's location."

Chip pushed open the dining room door from the kitchen. "You need me to come along."

"No, stay here with the kids. If it turns into something, I'll let you know. You've got a houseful of people to keep track of."

Chip nodded and ducked back into the kitchen to finish up in there.

Ingrid said, "This Warren, is he someone you trust?"

"Definitely. But with a houseful of people and a few demons, Chip should stay here."

"Mind if I tag along? I have a feeling you might have need of me, and I think you and I should come to an understanding concerning the current situation."

That didn't sound great. I also knew if I turned her down, she'd likely just follow me on her own. Eldara were very resourceful. It was a good idea to come to an understanding of what she was and wasn't willing to do about this demon incursion.

"Sure, come along. Warren's my investigator—and a werewolf. If you're okay with that, you're welcome to join me."

"Gibson," Ingrid said. "You can return to Elk City. I will remain in Westminster for the time being."

"If you say so. It would be nice to get back to Hangbe. She's only in town for a few more days. I'll say goodbye to Sadie and Chip and get on the road. If you need me, you know where to find me."

I said goodbye to Sadie. "Keep an eye on your uncle. I'll be back soon."

"It just feels good to be out from under Gorrath's influence. Now I can lend a hand in the fight without worrying I'm going to suddenly become a liability."

"Just stay here and don't turn your back on the company." I glanced at Azith and Dezik. The pair stood together by the sofa in the next room, watching everyone else in silence. I didn't trust them.

"Ready?" I asked Ingrid.

"Lead on, arms-mistress."

I appreciated the recognition of my place in the family hierarchy. "My car's out front."

Ingrid followed me outside and waited by the passenger side of the Firebird until I unlocked the door from the inside. She climbed in and fastened her seat belt. I couldn't hide a chuckle when she buckled up.

"You find my presence amusing?"

"No, it's just funny that you buckle your seatbelt. You're damned near immortal. I wouldn't think a thing like a motor vehicle accident would be something you'd be afraid of."

"You're correct about the almost immortal nature of the Eldara. However, it's a case of observing local laws and ordinances. We wouldn't want to get pulled over because I wasn't restrained."

"Fair enough." I started the car and pulled away from the curb, swinging around in a tight U-turn and accelerating out of the suburban neighborhood.

Warren waited for us in Johansen's, downtown by the railroad tracks. It was late, and I found a parking spot on the street out front.

Ingrid followed me inside as I peered through the dim lighting of the basement bar.

The werewolf leaned out from his spot in a booth near the rear of the room. He knew how to find a table where we would be unlikely to be overheard.

He gestured to the bench seat across from him and nodded at Ingrid. "Who's your divine friend?"

Warren didn't miss much, and his wolf senses likely pegged Ingrid as an Eldara as soon as she walked in.

"This is Ingrid. Chip called in a favor from his cousin and got us some help from one of the Valkyries."

That raised Warren's eyebrows. "Welcome to our corner of the New World, Ingrid. I hope you enjoy the little bit of excitement we're able to provide you."

"A demon incursion like this hasn't happened for a very long time. If one of the demon lords seeks to begin the wars of the Dark Ages again, it would be unfortunate, to say the least."

"That's what we're here to stop," I said. "What did you find out?"

Warren looked around and leaned over the table, keeping his voice down. "I found them."

"The cult? Are you sure?"

"I was finally able to track down the shell companies that own the temple land. They led back to a businessman here in Westminster. He owns several local convenience stores around the county, as well as a party supplies store in the mall. I checked on the mini-marts, and they're all pretty small. Mostly just gas stations with some snacks and sodas."

"What about the store in the mall here in Westminster?" I asked.

"That's where this gets interesting. It's been closed down for several days. Security doors are shut across the entrance, and I can't see inside. There's a 'closed for remodeling' sign taped to the outside with no other explanations."

"It's not unusual for stores to remodel," Ingrid said. "What makes you think this might be where they're hiding out now?"

"I checked with a friend who works security at the mall. They usually get a heads up when a store is doing construction work. The guards sometimes have to let contractors in for their work before the mall opens in the morning. They've got nothing like that on the books for the party shop. There was just the printed sign on the outside one morning when they did their security checks."

"When was this?"

"Right after you all raided the temple." Warren smiled. "It all fits."

"Yes, it does." I didn't bother to hide my smile.

"Excellent," Ingrid said. "Then we raid this mall location and deal with the demon worshipers. Such riff-raff is better dealt with sooner than later."

"We can't charge in blind," I said. "I want to know what they're planning first."

Ingrid glared at me. "You say you wish to combat this evil, and yet you hesitate when we finally track them down. Are you as resolute as you say you are?"

"I'm resolute up to the point where innocent people are put in danger. It's late. Let's come up with a viable plan first, then approach them from a position of strength."

"Ladies, it doesn't matter what you want. I can't get us in there until tomorrow morning at the earliest. My friend won't be back at work until six a.m. He can unlock the loading-dock door for us to slip in. Then we should be able to come at them from behind."

Ingrid tapped the table with one finger a few times. "That may be a better solution. If we enter before the mall opens for patrons, we could overcome the cultists before there's any risk to the public."

I smirked. "See, that wasn't so bad, was it?"

"I still prefer a direct approach, but this will do. This kind of plan is much more the kind of thing my sister would consider if she were here directing things."

"I think I'd like to meet her sometime," I said. "Is she a Valkyrie like you?"

"No, she is one of the Eldara sisters. She currently works as a nurse in Elk City."

I was impressed. I didn't know one of the legendary healing Eldara was living so close. Of course, I didn't know there was an actual Valkyrie staying an hour and a half from home either.

"Warren," I said. "Reach out to your friend. Make sure he can let us in first thing in the morning. Don't let on there might be a fight. I don't want any interference from him or his fellow guards."

"I don't know, Rose. It might be a good idea to let him know something is up. He could run interference for us with the other security goons. I trust him to keep this on the down-low."

"I could wipe his memory," Ingrid offered. "Once we recover Gorrath, I could make sure he has no recollection of our arrival or any conflict that might erupt around the cultists."

"How reliable is that?" I asked.

"Very, and for such a short time period, there would be very few side effects. He and his fellow guards would likely not even notice they missed the time when I release them from the spell."

I considered the possibilities for a few seconds and nodded. "Do it. If things go sideways, I want their memories clean. We'll have to do something if we have any injuries or—worse yet—bodies to hide."

"Good," Warren said. "I'm glad we have that worked out. I'll contact him now. How many people are we expecting to show up for this? Just you two?"

"We'll probably bring Chip along. The kids will be going to school, but he may have them see themselves off if there's a chance for some action."

"What about the two demons?" Ingrid asked. "They may interfere rather than help us in a fight. I can't help but think they have their own agenda for Gorrath."

"I think we drop them back off at their hiding place near the high school for now. Both of them are injured anyway, so they wouldn't be much help in a fight." I pointed to Ingrid. "You can definitely tell if Gorrath is there once we're close enough, right?"

"Of yes. I have the taste of him and will sense him when we draw near. We'll know when we arrive at the mall in the morning."

"Good, then contact your friend, Warren. We'll return to Chip's and fill him in on the plan."

I slid out of the booth, followed by Ingrid. Warren sipped at the remaining half of his beer. "I'll see you ladies by the loading dock behind the mall tomorrow. Let's make it six thirty. That'll give him some time to make sure no one else is around before we get there."

I nodded and walked out. Ingrid might be on our side—for now. But if push came to shove, I wasn't sure where her loyalty would fall. The divine don't always care who they step on to win.

Ingrid said, "It is strange you put so much faith in a shifter when your Fae background should prevent you from trusting them."

"I've known Warren a very long time. I'd trust him with my life. He'll get things set up for us. Don't worry."

"Good, I'd hate for us to gear up for a fight and then nothing happens. It's been too long since I've had a good battle with a demon lord."

I held back on the eye roll. After all, I'd brought a Valkyrie to the battle this time. I just wasn't sure which side she'd be on when the blood started flowing.

22

Chip

"Okay, Sadie, you have everything you need to go back to school this morning. I put the note from the doctor on the counter beside your backpack. It gives you permission to come back to school and to practice with the team again, too. Don't forget it."

"I won't, Uncle Chip. Can't I come with you, though? I should see this through."

"Me, too," Addy said. "I want to fight the demon cult."

"You've helped a lot already, but this one's for the grown-ups. We'll fill you in after. Besides, it's probably going to be boring. They won't be expecting us. We might show up and be able to steal the ball back without a fight."

"Are you taking anyone else with you besides Aunt Rose and Ingrid?" Sadie asked.

"I think Warren will be there. Gwinn and Hitch went home together last night. It looks like they patched things up between themselves for now. We're going to drop Azith and Dezik off in town before we go over to the mall."

"What if the four of you aren't enough?" Sadie's hopeful eyes carried a wish to come along.

"Then we'll back off and figure out another way in. I appreciate you've been such good helpers already, but let us do the grown-up stuff when we need to."

Both kids deflated a little and returned to their breakfasts. I knew they'd get over it. They both enjoyed their time at school and their friends, and it was important for them to be somewhere they would be safe.

I went to the family room, where Dezik and Azith had sat all night. It was strange. They didn't seem to sleep and appeared to be in the same positions they were in when I left them to go make breakfast.

Azith faced me when I approached. "Your niece is correct. You should take us along in case you need assistance in recovering Gorrath from the cultists."

"Both of you are wounded. I'm afraid I'd spend more time worrying about you than relying on your help." I didn't add that having along demons with a separate agenda made that spot between my shoulder blades itch. It was best to return them to their playing field hideout beneath the stands. They could best serve us as lookouts for anything strange coming from the portal.

The front door opened, and Rose came in, followed by Warren. She held up a plastic bag. "I got a burner phone. I figured Azith and Dezik can use it to contact us if anything happens at the field."

"Good idea. You guys understand how to use a phone to communicate, don't you?"

Azith glanced at Dezik. "I think we can learn fast enough."

Rose removed the plastic packaging the phone came in. It was an old-style flip phone. She turned it on and fiddled with it for a minute, then came over.

"I've programmed my number and Chip's into the phone." Rose walked them through the basics—names, green button to call, red to hang up.

Dezik caught on quickly and called me, amazed at the clarity. "Remarkable. And you can hear me over there?"

I nodded. "Yes, I can. Now press the red button to disconnect."

Dezik looked down at the phone in his hand and tapped a button, and the call ended. "This is truly a wondrous device."

Azith said, "This would have been useful when we first arrived and started searching for Gorrath while separated. We spent much time retracing our steps to meet up and give each other a report of our progress."

I grinned. "I'm glad we can impress you. Dibs on the cell tower contracts in hell."

Rose glowered at me. "That's not funny. No one should ever enter into a contract with the nether powers."

"It was a joke, Rose." I slid my phone back into my pants pocket. "Okay, we're all here."

"Where's Ingrid?"

"I'm here." She jogged down the stairs from the bathroom upstairs, where she had asked to freshen up. She carried the glowing silver short sword in one hand. There was no scabbard on her belt that I could see.

"You might want to put that away. If someone sees it, there're going to be awkward questions."

"Put what away?" Ingrid asked.

I blinked. Her hand was empty.

Right. Valkyrie magic.

Rose chuckled. "It's all part of the Eldara schtick."

Ingrid said, "It's useful to have weapons immediately handy, but not evident to all who watch."

"I won't argue with that." I hooked a thumb over my shoulder. "Shall we load up in the SUV?"

"Warren will go with you," Rose said. "Ingrid can ride with me in the Firebird. We'll follow you."

"Good enough. Azith, Dezik, ready to go?"

Both demons stood. Their human forms could definitely use a bath and a fresh change of clothes, but hopefully they'd only be here for another day at the most. I led them and Warren out through the garage entrance in the kitchen, and we loaded up the SUV.

Morning traffic was heavy. It took us over twenty minutes to navigate across town to the high school playing fields and the main grandstands. I pulled into the empty lot and stopped beside the field house.

"Use the phone if you see anything we need to know about."

Azith nodded. "We would appreciate if you likewise kept us apprised of your progress."

"Fair enough." I waited for the two to exit the back seat, then pulled away from the parking lot.

Rose followed right behind me in the red Firebird. Next up was the mall. I hoped it would be the beginning of the end of our adventure with Gorrath.

It didn't take us long to pull into the rear parking lot at the mall. A line of three loading docks for trailer trucks faced us as we parked. An employee entrance lay to the right of the freight doors.

I got out with Warren and walked over to where Rose and Ingrid stood beside the Firebird. "So, ladies, what's the plan?" I unclipped the hilt from my belt and hoped the answer wasn't to kick in the door and go in with our blades held high.

Rose drew her sword and dropped the scabbard on the Firebird's front seat. "Ingrid will take the lead."

"Yes, I can sense the demon lord's presence from out here. It should be of little trouble to locate him once I'm inside the building."

A voice called out from over by the mall. "Warren." A man in a tan security uniform held open the door at the employee entrance.

Rose held her sword at her side. "Lead on, Warren. This is your guy."

The werewolf led us across the parking lot to the entrance.

"Hey, Dirk. Any activity around that party store this morning?"

"No, it's quiet, but the lights have been on all night, and now and then, I can see shapes moving around behind the translucent barrier. There are people in there."

"Good. We'll take it from here." Warren gestured for Ingrid and Rose to enter past him. "Make sure you keep the other guards down at the far end of the mall."

"You won't see them. I had a dozen donuts delivered to the security office, along with a box of fresh coffee. They won't be out for a while. The only other people in there are the early morning mall walkers. Most are senior citizens who can't hear very well. They shouldn't bother you unless you open the gate at the front of the store."

"Good. I'll pay you back for the donuts. Now go join them. We'll be finished here quickly. By the time you come back, everything will be over."

Dirk looked over his shoulder in both directions and leaned close to Warren. "There won't be any bodies to clean up, will there? I can't cover for that kind of thing."

"No worries there. You won't have any bodies to worry about."

I didn't know how Warren could promise that, but I left it alone. We needed this guard to relax and let us do our thing.

Dirk relaxed and blew out a sigh. "Good. Those two ladies looked ready for trouble. Was that one carrying a sword?"

"It's just decorative," I suggested. "That's all."

"Oh, good. Okay. Call me if you need me sooner. I need to hurry before all the donuts are gone."

Dirk disappeared inside, and Warren and I followed down a long, plain hallway with doors on the righthand side. Each was labeled with a store name. This was the rear area for all the stores on this side of the mall. Dirk turned down a side branch of the hallway and disappeared. We kept walking until we spotted Ingrid and Rose standing outside a door labeled "Party Place."

Ingrid raised her hand, and the glowing sword flashed into place. "Gorrath is inside. I can feel his ilk behind this door."

Rose drew her blade, and I squeezed the leather-wrapped hilt in my hand. I'd extend the blade when I needed it. It would only get in the way in the meantime. Warren bared his teeth in a grin that revealed enlarged canines. His nails had lengthened to one-inch claws beyond his fingertips.

"I guess we're ready, then." I reached for the door and tried the knob. It was locked.

Ingrid grinned and leaned back, planting her booted foot against the door beside the knob, kicking it in with no trouble. She followed the buckling door with a bellowing war cry.

Rose followed, then Warren.

I brought up the rear.

We charged through a storage area full of floor-to-ceiling shelves and past a checkout counter to enter the main store area. The center of the floor had been cleared of shelves to create a roundish temple area.

The soccer ball rested on a chrome-and-glass pedestal that used to hold some store display. Eight robed cultists knelt on the carpeted floor around the pedestal. All had twisted to look in our direction, following Ingrid's loud entrance.

The Valkyrie jumped up on the sales counter and leaped over the nearest worshipers toward the soccer ball demon.

The closest worshiper grabbed for her. Her blade flashed, and a severed hand flew away in a spray of blood.

The cultist fell back. He clutched at his bloody stump and screamed.

Ingrid landed where he'd knelt seconds before and swept the shining silver sword around to clear the area.

Rose ran in to stand at her back as the other worshipers drew wicked curved knives from their robes and rushed at the two women.

"I guess we should try to circle around to get to the soccer ball." I slid to the side with Warren and went to the left, past the stacked store shelves along the wall. The melee in the center kept me pressed against the side as I tried to go behind the cultists circling the two women.

Warren's shout alerted me. "Hey, Chip, that one's getting away with the ball."

A robed cultist had grabbed Gorrath from the pedestal and was running for the front of the store. The translucent chain-and-plastic barrier was closed, so I didn't know where he was going.

I ran after the guy.

He raced up to a control panel and pressed a button. The barrier retracted into the walls. A gap opened, and six gray-haired seniors shuffled in. Their eyes were completely white with no pupils. Gorrath had them under his spell.

The cultist darted past them and disappeared into the mall. More and more of the mall walkers entered, all moaning incoherently. They didn't attack, but they filled the store's narrow exit like a human barricade—slow-moving, but impenetrable.

"Warren," I called. "Can you get around them? I don't want to hurt anyone. It's not their fault they've been possessed."

The werewolf ran to the far side, but the mall walkers blocked him, too. There was no way past them unless I was willing to start chopping them down with my blade.

Behind us, the two women had finished the rest of the cultists. All the robed figures were down. Rose knelt beside one who only had a gash across his shoulder. He fought to rise, but she held the guy down easily.

The milling mall walkers didn't advance beyond the entrance. They clearly had their instructions and were doing an excellent job of blocking the pursuit of the demon-possessed ball.

Ingrid joined Rose with the only surviving cultist. She knelt down beside the wounded man. "Where is your companion taking Gorrath?"

"To complete the plan. You cannot stop the great demon lord."

Ingrid squeezed his injured shoulder until he screamed. "What plan? Tell me. I won't kill you. I'll just drag you into the higher planes for my fellow Eldara to practice their torture on you."

"You don't scare me. It's too late. The plan has already been set in motion. Soon Gorrath's legions from hell will spill into this world to begin a new dominion over everyone."

"I don't have time for this," Ingrid said. She flicked her wrist, making the sword disappear from her hand. Then she gripped the cultist's head and tilted his face up so he had to stare into her eyes. They flashed with silver light.

"Tell. Me. The. Plan."

The man tried to wrench his head free, but the Valkyrie held on. "Tell me the plan. You cannot resist me."

He let out a yowl. Words spilled from his mouth. "Tonight, the Great Lord will feast on the souls of the fallen! The coach is merely his vessel. Victory on the field will be our trumpet blast—a signal to hell that the gates to this plane are open!"

Before I could ask what on earth he was talking about, Rose said, "He must mean they've gotten to the coach of Liberty High."

"Who is that?" Ingrid asked.

"The visiting team Sadie is playing against tonight. They're from the other end of the county."

"Sadie's team can't stand up to demon-enhanced players," I said. "What do we do?"

"We go home and come up with a plan to stop him. Failure is not an option. Ingrid, do we still have your help in this quest?"

"I came to root out this infestation. I will go with you and lend what aid I can during this contest tonight."

Rose nodded. She looked around and pointed at the rear of the store. "We have to prepare a plan. I don't know exactly how, but we have to stop Gorrath."

I glanced around at the bodies strewn around the floor and the still-groggy mall walkers. "What about all the carnage? We promised Dirk there wouldn't be any bodies."

Warren herded the aimlessly shuffling mall walkers toward the store's entrance. "I'll take care of it. There's a clean-up crew on speed dial. I've been working with Rose for a long time now. We know what needs doing." He waited until the final white-haired mall walker moseyed into the mall proper and pressed the button to close the barrier before they came back to their senses.

Rose and Ingrid nodded to each other and led the way out.

I followed, casting one last look at the carnage behind us. Tonight, hell was coming to a high school soccer pitch. We'd better be ready.

23

Rose

My gut told me to keep Sadie home from the game tonight. We'd lock the doors, draw the curtains, and ride out whatever hell Gorrath had planned. But I knew better. Destiny didn't wait for the cautious, and Sadie had a role to play, whether or not I liked it.

Plus, we had an Eldara on our side. Ingrid gave us advantages Gorrath wouldn't be expecting.

I left my Firebird behind for Warren to bring back when he finished with the cleanup at the mall. It wasn't my first choice, but he would be careful with my car. I rode back with Chip and Ingrid.

The fight had made me hungry. "Chip, you have anything for a brunch at the house? I'm starving."

He glanced over at me in the passenger seat. His face had turned a little green. "I don't know how you could be hungry after all that."

Ingrid leaned forward between the seats. "A victory feast is an excellent idea. I, too, am famished."

"Uh, okay," Chip said. "I have eggs and bacon. There's some left-over baguette, too, so I could make some French toast on the side. How does that sound?"

Ingrid sat back in her seat. "Perfect. I hope you have enough. I have mana to replenish."

Chip looked back at her through the rearview mirror. "I thought you drew upon the gods or whatever for power."

"My mandate comes from the gods of the light. However, I carry my own store of energy for battle. If there is to be a fight tonight, I must be ready." The fire burned in her eyes in a way that told me she looked forward to the conflict.

Maybe I needed to douse the fire a little. "Perhaps we should come up with a way to stop it before it happens. We don't want open war on the soccer pitch tonight."

"I don't think we can stop this from happening," Ingrid said. "In my bones, it has the feel of a foretold event."

My mind went back to my encounter with the gangster oracle. Her prophecy had connected Sadie with the demon ball.

I kept the oracle's prediction to myself for the time being. There was a decision to be made about whether to trust Ingrid with Sadie's secret or not.

I was inclined to trust her. After all, if you couldn't trust one of the heavenly messengers, who could you trust? It wasn't a decision I could make alone, though. Chip had a say, as much as it irked me. He was the Guardian in the end.

We arrived back at the house, and I helped Chip prep the brunch while he cooked. I'd had his French toast before. It was a delight. The guy was a pretty decent cook.

It didn't take him long to whip up a delicious late-morning feast for us. He even sat down and dug in with gusto, despite his initial reaction to the idea.

Ingrid noticed his appetite, too. "I thought you weren't hungry, Chip."

"The fight back at the mall wasn't pretty, but you're right. There's something about needing food after that kind of adrenaline surge."

"It is the gods' way of demonstrating you survived and are still alive. I've seen it many times over the millennia I've served. Humans crave food following a battle."

"Does that mean I'll need to prepare a feast for tonight after the game as well? We can't avoid that fight."

"Maybe we can settle for some late-night carryout," I said. "Before we can order it, though, we have to win."

"What did you have in mind?" Ingrid asked. "I fear the mundane humans of this time are ill-equipped to be involved with this kind of fight. No one believes in demons anymore."

"That's why we have to help Sadie's team win tonight."

"You want to take her there?" Chip asked. "Won't that be dangerous?"

"I don't think we can avoid it. Ingrid is right about people and their inability to fend off demonic possession—or even influence. The only way to combat it is to have a powerful champion for the light there to fight back."

Ingrid shoved a piece of syrup-laden French toast into her mouth and shook her head. She swallowed and said, "I can lend aid, but I cannot be your champion. It has long been the rule that humans and the other denizens of earth must find their own victors in contests like this."

"Who, then?" Chip asked. "I suppose I could step up, but I know nothing about fighting demons."

"Not you, Chip. Sadie."

"How can the girl be your champion?" Ingrid looked back and forth between us, confused. "I broke the tie between them. She should be free of this."

I glanced at Chip. We were standing on the edge of something we couldn't undo. Once Ingrid knew the truth, there'd be no going back.

"Can we trust you, Ingrid? Trust you with our greatest secret?"

"I will not divulge any confidence you share with me, even unto death."

I didn't point out that she was immortal. After waiting for Chip's nod of assent, I said, "Sadie is in line to be the next Fae queen. She will come into her full power in three years on her eighteenth birthday. But she is not without considerable resources even now."

Ingrid smiled. "Wild magic? That changes everything. Yes, with that kind of power, she could sway the entire match."

"I was hoping you could help us with that side of things. We've never asked her to use her power in this kind of event."

"When Gorrath first came and was trapped inside the ball, Sadie wasn't affected, nor were those closest to her," Ingrid said. "That means her energy innately protected those around her. I think that's the key to winning this fight."

"If I understand you right," Chip said, "you're proposing Sadie draw in enough power to extend protection to the whole stadium?"

"No." Ingrid used her knife to gesture while she talked. "This will be a contest between the two teams alone. One team will be Gorrath's, and his possession of the players on his side will be total. She must pass her protection on to all the players on her side."

That made me sit back and think. Sadie's mere presence was enough to protect those within about fifteen feet of her. The field was way bigger than that. She'd have to expand her protection exponentially to cover that much ground.

"The field's too big," I said after thinking about it. "Even if she could amplify her power, Gorrath's influence will be thick over the field. Wild magic doesn't like being tangled with dark energy. She'll need help broadcasting it."

"You're thinking too literally, Rose." Chip's eyes had a mischievous light in them. "In all the adventure movies, the heroes share a cup or meal together beforehand to cement their victory. We just need her to infuse enough of her protection into some vessel and have the team share in it before the game."

"A victory potion?" My eyes narrowed. "That would take some work, and I don't think any of us here possess the skills to make one in the short time we have."

"Easy," Chip said. "We just ask Hitch and Gwinn to come back. Together, they can whip up something."

"It's not that easy, Chip." I shook my head. "In order to work the magic into the formula, they'd have to understand how Sadie was drawing on all that power. It would be hard to keep them from figuring out how she did it."

Ingrid chuckled. "If you played for the other side, you'd just kill them after they brew the potion."

"Well, we can't do that," I said. "We've left enough bodies in our wake already. Even though they were evil cultists, their disappearance will cause an investigation. Warren has his hands full enough."

Chip shrugged. "We tell them."

"Chip, I don't think that's the answer."

"Rose, we can't protect her secret forever. We told Ingrid. Why not them? In three years, the whole Unusual community will know who she is. It's time we let a few more into the inner circle. Besides, isn't Hitch deathly afraid of you?"

I smiled. "He is, but Gwinn's another story. She's not tied to the family the way Hitch has become over the years."

"What if she were?"

I cocked my head to the side and stared at Chip.

"Stay with me here," he said. "Gwinn is trying to separate from the local coven. They frown on unattached witches operating in the community. What if she weren't unattached?"

I saw where he was going. It might work. A court witch with Gwinn's talents could make the difference, not just tonight, but in the years to come. If she agreed.

"Gwinn would have to accept a position as the queen's witch. That's risky. She might say no. She'd be giving up one tie that binds her for another."

"Come on," he said with a big grin. "This is negotiation 101. I'll make her think it was her idea by the time I'm finished. She'll be begging to be Sadie's personal witch."

As much as I didn't want to buy into Chip's enthusiasm, he was probably right. My brother-in-law could sell ice cubes on a glacier. He'd make this the most desirable outcome for everyone.

I texted Hitch.

> Is Gwinn still with you?

> Yes, why?

> Where are you? Chip and I need to come see you both. It's important.

> We're at my apartment.

We'll be right over.

I SLID the phone into my back pocket. "Let's go. I can't believe I'm saying this, but it's time for you to put that old Chipster charm back into action. I hope you still have it."

He flashed me a grin. "Why, Rose, I'll never run out of that. I'll even save some just for you." He winked.

I mimed shoving a finger in my throat.

We laughed, but the truth was serious. Tonight, a teenage girl would face down a demon lord. And we were going to make damn sure she didn't do it alone.

24

Chip

I worked through my approach to Gwinn while we drove downtown to Hitch's apartment over a store on Main Street. We got lucky with a spot on the street.

Rose waited at the curb for me to join her. "Chip, we need both Gwinn and Hitch to buy into this. You'll have to make this negotiation work out for the two of them in a way that satisfies their separate interests."

"That won't be too hard. Hitch is easy. He's a mercenary and all about the money. We offer him a position that comes with some opportunities for wealth, and he'll jump at the chance. Gwinn, though, is trickier. I don't think she's motivated by the same things as Hitch. Follow my lead with her. Once we get her on board, we can bring Hitch along with the right cash offer."

"Just remember anything you offer you have to explain to Aunt Allura. She's the holder of the purse strings in the family."

"Don't worry about that. I have plenty of extra on my side. We'll get Hitch on board." I looked down the street. "Which one is it, again?"

"Follow me."

Rose led me to a door beside a store selling musical instruments. She reached out to press the buzzer on the panel by the door.

I tapped her on the shoulder and pointed. "The door's open." I pushed it, and it popped off the partially closed latch with ease.

"Stay behind me, Chip. Sometimes Hitch gets himself in trouble, and I have to deal with his more unsavory acquaintances."

I waved for her to go first, and she walked up the two steps to the doorway and inside to a narrow staircase up to the second floor. The place was a dump, but that didn't surprise me for Hitch. I didn't see Gwinn being very comfortable here, though.

Rose stopped outside one of the apartment doors on the second floor. She rapped on it twice with her knuckles.

Hitch's muffled voice filtered out from inside. "Come in, Rose. It's open."

Rose opened the door and started to go inside. A flash of light glinted off iridescent lavender hair beside the door.

"Rose, watch out!"

I yanked her arm, pulling her back right before a jet of magical blue flame scorched the door frame where her face had been seconds before.

Geraldine, one of the witches who'd attacked Gwinn at the coffee shop, stepped into the doorway. Her hands worked together, forming an intricate weave of gestures as she glared at us.

On pure instinct, I raised my Guardian barrier between us and the witch. Then I had an idea and curved the invisible force field like a parabolic dish facing back at Geraldine.

The purple-haired witch released another spell. More of the blue magic fire jetted out at us.

Six inches from my face, it splashed against the curved surface of my barrier and splattered back on its sender.

Geraldine screamed and staggered backward, batting at the smoldering patches of magic in her hair and on her black coat.

Rose took a step to go inside after her, but I stopped her.

"Watch out. There's a pair of them."

On cue, Emi, the shorter blonde witch, pushed around her distracted companion and shouted, "Electramus!"

A bolt of lightning shot from her extended finger right at us.

Once again, the barrier's curve worked to our advantage. It not only blocked the magical lightning but directed it back at the caster.

Emi yelped and dove to the floor just in time to avoid the returning electricity. It impacted the far wall, creating a smoldering crater in the plaster and wooden lathe beneath it.

Rose pulled out of my grasp and ran around my shield. She raced inside. Without slowing at all, she spun in a roundhouse kick that caught the recovering Geraldine across the side of her head.

The witch's head snapped around, spittle flying from her slackened mouth. Her eyes rolled up in her head, and she flopped to the floor.

The angry Fae princess charged at the blonde witch, who crab walked backward to get away from her. Her back met the wall, and she winced when Rose cocked back a fist to throw a finishing blow.

To my surprise, Rose held her punch in place beside her head.

"Give me one good reason I don't punch your lights out right now, Emi Ward."

"Rose, I'm sorry. I didn't know it was you. We just knew someone was coming to meet the mage."

"Not good enough, Emi. Maybe I should tell Jessica about you and your friend attacking random people with magic in public."

Emi shook her head. "No, it was an honest mistake. We're just here to bring Gwinn back to face justice from the coven for violating our rules. You're here for the mage, right?"

"Unfortunately for you, we're here for both of them."

I stepped up to the doorway and looked around. Hitch and Gwinn were bound with duct tape, sitting back-to-back on the floor in the far corner. I reached into my pocket and pulled out my penknife.

While Rose towered over the fallen Emi, I flicked open the blade and cut the tape binding their hands. Both quickly freed themselves.

Hitch pointed at Emi. "They attacked us, Rose. Then you texted, and they lured you here. They knew it was you. They laughed about it."

Rose didn't hesitate. She punched Emi twice in the face and stood up. The blonde witch slumped over, unconscious. "I knew it. Emi used to be one of Patty's mean girls in high school. She hasn't changed at all."

"I'm glad you're here," Gwinn said. "That's twice you've helped me out of a bind, Chip."

"That's what friends do, Gwinn. You've helped us, too."

Rose looked around and located the duct tape on the kitchen table. She made quick work of binding the hands, feet, and mouths of the unconscious witches. Then she dragged them over to the floor inside the door. A quick check of the hallway to make sure no one else was out there, and she closed it.

"No sense getting the neighbors involved," Rose said. "Now, where were we? Ah, yes, we were at the part where you owe me one, Hitch. Again."

Her takeover of my carefully planned pitch annoyed me. "Rose, that's no way to talk to Hitch. He's been an immense help to us over the years."

She glared at me for a second.

I returned her gaze with an icy glare of my own.

She gave a single quick nod. "Fine. This is your show, Chip."

"What's she talking about?" Gwinn asked.

"What she's talking about is we need your help, and I think we might have a way to help you, too."

Gwinn walked with Hitch over to the ratty plaid sofa and sat down. "Okay, we're listening. What do you want?"

"It's more about what you want," I began. "Geraldine and Emi here will not give up. And Rose and I won't always be around to help."

Hitch said, "We can handle ourselves."

"Sure—but wouldn't it be nice to have our protection full-time?"

Gwinn's eyebrows pinched. "You just said you can't be around wherever I go. Eventually, they'll catch up with me."

"Not if they're told to lay off," I replied.

Hitch shook his head. "How are you going to do that? You don't have any pull with the coven. Jessica rules them with an iron fist."

"She does, and she knows Rose protects her family the same way."

"What do Rose and her family have to do with the coven?" Gwinn asked. "Jessica doesn't particularly like the Fae and their air of superiority. She says so all the time."

Rose moved to stand beside me. "Once Jessica knows you're under the family's aegis, she won't touch you. Coven law forbids it. She might hate me, but she respects the power behind our name."

"What Rose is trying to say is, if you want, we could extend the family protection to you—both of you."

"Why would you do that?" asked Hitch. "What's in it for you?"

I knew how to grab his attention. "How'd you like to be on retainer, Hitch? A regular monthly payment that would cover any magical spell and protection charm needs we might have?"

"Allura's tight with the money. Rose has said as much. How are you going to get her to pay for that?"

"She'd do it if she thought there was a long-term benefit to her niece."

Hitch didn't get it. "Who? Rose?"

"No." I shook my head. "Sadie. You'd serve her, not Rose."

"She's just a kid. Why would I do that?"

I rolled my eyes. Hitch could be more than a little thick-headed sometimes. He was useful, but not always terribly intuitive. I caught a glint in Gwinn's eyes, though.

The young witch tapped her chin. "We'd serve the girl. But for how long?"

"As long as you and she keep your oaths to each other."

Gwinn smiled. I knew she'd figured it out.

Hitch, on the other hand, still hadn't. "Why would I swear an oath to a fifteen-year-old girl?"

Gwinn nudged him with an elbow. "You wouldn't be swearing to a teenage girl. You'd be swearing to the future Fae queen." She met my eyes. "I'm right, aren't I? It's the only thing that makes sense."

"You just figured out a secret that I've killed to keep hidden for the last fifteen years," Rose said. "You understand what it would mean if you swore an oath to Sadie. You'd take the secret to the grave or pay the price."

Hitch stared at Rose, finally putting all the years of services and spells together. "Ohhhh, so much makes sense now. I've been serving her all along, haven't I?"

"In your own pig-headed way," Rose said. "But now you know the secret. I'm not sure you're up to keeping it."

"He'll keep it." Gwinn said. "He proposed to me this morning. I'm in, and that will bind him as well. On my life."

I smiled. I'd just closed the deal for both of them. The old Chipster still had it.

"Honey," Hitch said. "Are you sure? This is probably forever."

"It's better than having to move away and worry about the next coven discovering me in another town. This way I get to stay close to home and still practice my arts."

Hitch shrugged. "I guess I'm in, too. You've got yourself a court mage—with a commensurate retainer, of course."

"You'll get your money, Hitch," Rose said. "But you don't get it until she's crowned. That means you have a stake in keeping her safe for the next three years until she's on the throne."

"No money at all?" Hitch whined.

I said, "You'll get paid for each job for the next little while, the way we've always handled you. Otherwise, people might put two and two together. Once she's had her coronation, everyone will know you've been in her service for years. That alone should be worth a lot."

"It definitely is," Gwinn answered. She turned and gripped Hitch's hands in her own. "Take the oath with me right now. Then when she's crowned, Sadie can marry us. We'll be specially blessed because of it."

Hitch gulped. He might have wanted to marry this girl, but suddenly his entire future had come into focus. I didn't think he minded, though. It was just a lot to take in.

He squeezed her hands in his and nodded.

I glanced at Gwinn and Hitch, hands clasped, pledging their future to a fifteen-year-old girl who hadn't yet reached the throne. Sadie wasn't just gaining allies. She was gaining devotion.

"So, what do you need us to do?" Gwinn asked. "You didn't come here without a good reason."

Rose moved over to where the two bound witches lay on the floor.

"Help me drag these two into the hallway. Then come with us. I'll call Jessica and notify her you're with us. She can come and pick them up.

Hitch walked over to help Rose with Geraldine. I motioned for Gwinn to help me with Emi.

"We'll fill you in about what we need on the way back to the house," I said. "There's a lot we have to do before tonight's soccer game."

I glanced at the unconscious witches one last time.

"Because if we don't get this right, we're not just losing the game—we're losing the whole damn town."

Rose

It didn't take Gwinn and Hitch long to prove their worth, confirming the wisdom of Chip's insistence on their long-term service to Sadie. By midafternoon, they'd come up with a way to use Sadie's wild magic in a spell-based potion to empower her team with her royal Fae protection.

Halfway through the process, Ingrid left to scout the high school, agreeing to return in time to update us on the situation there. While I worried she might take matters into her own hands before we could arrive, my place was here to ensure Sadie was safe.

Chip came up with the perfect delivery method. He snapped his fingers while we were deep in the planning stages and left the kitchen to root around in the garage. He returned with the large orange five-gallon water cooler. We could fill it with a sports drink, or even a magic potion, and set it up for the team. We'd put it by the field, and Sadie would ensure everyone drank from it before the game. Most of the girls were good about hydrating, so they would partake of the potion without us having to force them.

Gwinn pointed at the counter. "Set it up over here by the stove. I'll work in this big stockpot, and then we'll ice the potion down before we pour it into the cooler."

Hitch stood beside Gwinn and handed her the potion ingredients one at a time from where he'd laid them out across the counter. He had gone earlier to the herbalist's stand next to the old orchards west of town and returned with a big cardboard box. I didn't recognize most of what he set out on the counter. There were many rare and obscure herbs in her concoction.

Gwinn supplemented Hitch's haul with a collection of bottles and vials she kept inside her leather shoulder bag, which I had assumed was just a big purse. Instead, it contained her key spell components.

She stirred the dry ingredients with a big wooden spoon, letting them toast first with no liquid. A pleasant, earthy scent wafted up as she mixed them over the heat. "Okay, it's ready. Hand me the jug of distilled water."

"Why not use water from the tap?" Chip asked.

I answered for Gwinn. "We don't want any random minerals contaminating the mix. It has to be as pure as possible."

Hitch poured the water in slowly while he watched Gwinn's face as she stirred the ingredients. She gave a curt nod, and Hitch lifted the plastic jug away from the hot pot.

She stirred a few more times and stepped back with her hands on her hips. "That'll have to do for now. It needs to simmer for a while. The next step involves Sadie. When is she home from school?"

Chip glanced at his watch. "The bus drops off in about a half hour. Should I have driven to school and picked them up?"

"No," Gwinn said. "Someone will have to stand here and stir the pot while we wait, though. There's no magic infused yet, but the mixture is persnickety and needs regular attention."

Hitch raised his hand. "I've got it. You rest. Once Sadie gets here, you're both going to need your energy."

The mage stepped in, took the big wooden spoon, and slowly stirred the warming mixture. A few wisps of steam rose now and then from the pot, but he was careful to keep the heat low so it didn't boil.

Gwinn left to go lie down on the sofa in the family room. I walked over to the kitchen table, where I'd left my sword. The long silver blade slid from its scabbard easily, and I sat down to run a whetstone along the edge. I honed it regularly and kept it razor sharp, so this was mostly to calm my nerves and help me focus on what was to come.

Thirty minutes later, the front door popped open and Sadie came in, followed by Addy. The middle school bus must have arrived with the high school bus. That happened sometimes.

I sheathed the sword and put the whetstone and honing oil back in its leather case and stood.

Sadie sniffed the air. "What's that wonderful smell? It's like all my favorite forest scents rolled into one massive candle."

"That's the potion we're cooking up for tonight's game." I pointed at Hitch, who still stirred the contents of the big stockpot by the stove.

Gwinn came in behind Sadie and stretched. "I feel much better. I think the tincture is ready now, too. Sadie, are you ready for some magical experimentation?"

Sadie's eyes lit up.

I held up a hand and stepped up by the stove. "Wait. I thought you knew what we needed to do. Now you're experimenting?"

"You think I've made a potion to protect a soccer team against a horde of demons before?" Her sarcasm dripped in the silence for a second.

I backed down. "Sorry, I'm worried about tonight. I guess I'd hoped there was more to this than a wild-assed guess."

Gwinn shrugged. "There's sound theory behind it. It should absolutely work. The biggest variable is Sadie. I've never worked with a primal source of wild magic before. It'll be new for all of us."

Something occurred to me. "Hey, if we're about to release that much wild magic energy, what about the emanations beyond the house? Will other Unusuals sense it in town?"

"Maybe—no, probably," Gwinn said. "Hitch, you might be able to mask it. You said you placed the protections on this house. Can you bolster them while I work with Sadie?"

"I suppose so," the mage said. "It depends on how much power we're talking about here."

"No way to know until Sadie and I work on imbuing the potion with the energy."

"Then all I can say is I'll do the best I can."

I didn't like it when Hitch hedged like that. He was good at what he did, despite all the other problems in his life. It was the reason I kept coming back to him. I had to trust him now.

"Do the best you can, Hitch. I believe you can do it."

Hitch's eyebrows raised. "Wow, a vote of confidence from you goes a long way, Rose. Thanks."

"Don't disappoint me." I didn't want his head getting too big. "Gwinn, what do you want Chip and me to do?"

"Chip, you keep Addy busy in the other room or, better yet, upstairs. He's got some power, too. I don't want him getting drawn into the energy exchange. This has to be all Sadie and me."

"And me?" I asked.

"Rose, you will stand by and be ready to add any more spell components as I call for them. I'll set out everything on the counter from my satchel next to the dry herbs."

I moved over to stand next to Gwinn. Sadie moved around to the witch's other side.

Chip walked over and nudged Addy. "Come on, bud. Let's go play something on the Xbox. The ladies have all this locked down in here."

"Aw, can't I stay and watch?"

"Nope. You heard Gwinn. Your awesome power might get mixed in and mess things up. Come on. We'll have fun while they do all the work."

The pair left through the door to the dining room, followed by Hitch.

"It's just us girls now," Gwinn said. "Okay, Sadie, when you draw upon your inner power with wild magic, what do you usually do?"

"I don't really play with it all that much. Most of my time is spent tamping it down inside where it won't get out. We had a problem a few years back with my magic."

"She had some control issues when it first showed up," I explained. "But you're older and more experienced now, Sadie. There have been no outbreaks in almost two years."

"Until now, when you ask me to let it all out." Sadie's voice quavered a little.

"Hey, this isn't some alien force. It's coming from inside you. *It is you.*"

"I get that, Aunt Rose, but I'm worried I'll lose control."

Gwinn smiled. "Think of it as opening a bathroom faucet. It's not like a dam bursting all at once. We're going to trickle it out at first. You'll have all the control you'll need."

"If you say so. Okay, what do I do?"

The witch started stirring until a little whirlpool appeared in the center of the pot. "Focus on the swirling liquid. Open up and let a little of your power out, directing it into the potion base as it trickles through you."

Sadie stared into the pot, and her intense eyes flared with the familiar sapphire light of her magic. This time, though, it flowed gently from her extended forefinger, her deep-blue mana-based power intertwined with streaks of gold and silver wild magic.

Inside the pot, the liquid sparkled with its own light. Gwinn hummed a crooning tune as her own nature magic released into the potion through the wooden spoon. A streak of pale green light swirled around and through Sadie's magical stream of blue, gold, and silver.

The hairs on my arm stood on end as the powerful flows of the two women increased in intensity.

In the next room, Hitch called out, "Whoa, easy ladies. That's a lot."

"Deal with it," I called out. "They're just getting started."

"Okay, Sadie," Gwinn said, "you've been opening it up slowly. Now's the time to cut it loose."

"I'm scared. Can't you do it, Aunt Rose?"

"We're both here for you, but it has to be you, hon. My power is a puddle next to the ocean you contain. Take a deep breath and focus. This is your power, no one else's."

Pride in my girl swelled when she nodded and drew her eyebrows down in concentration. She leaned over the pot and lowered her finger so it almost touched the surface of the whirlpool of liquid power inside.

"Here it comes."

I was not prepared for the rush of power that came from my niece.

The entire room shimmered as the magic supercharged the surrounding air. Waves of power thrummed through my body as Sadie's massive energy flowed out of her.

The house trembled. Lightbulbs dimmed, and even the refrigerator gave a groaning hum. The power gushing from Sadie didn't just fill the room—it seemed to press outward, brushing the limits of the house's protections.

The whole time, Gwinn's gentle humming croon never changed. It gave both Sadie and me something to hold on to in the midst of the energy storm growing from the pot.

Gwinn glanced away from the pot, searching. "Rose, I saw some oranges in the fridge earlier. Quick, cut a bunch in half and drop them in the pot."

I didn't waste time asking why. That could come later. I ran over to the refrigerator and pulled out a mesh bag of navel oranges. With a knife from the block on the counter, I sliced through the first orange and dropped it into the pot.

Instantly, a pleasant orange scent filled the air amidst the strong herbs.

"More," Gwinn said. "Go until you run out or I tell you to stop."

My hands moved with quick efficiency as I sliced more of the fruit in half and dropped the sections into the pot. Strangely, the level of the liquid didn't change, nor did I see any of the oranges floating inside as I tossed two more in. The orange scent grew, though, as the heavy herbal scent lessened.

I dropped in the last orange and stepped back. Gwinn's eyes glowed with pale green light as her humming increased in volume and intensity. Sadie's hair clung to her face, her skin sweat-soaked from the channeled power.

Sadie was giving too much of herself to this spell. There had to be another way to protect the town from the threatened demon incursion.

I was just about to reach out and pull her arm back from the pot when Gwinn removed the spoon from the mixture. She rapped once on the side with the spoon. A booming gonging sound came from inside.

"Sadie, step back. You can stop now. It's done."

"It is?" She wiped at the sweat that covered her face and forehead. "That was—I don't know—intense."

Gwinn laughed. She reached over and pulled Sadie close with an arm around her shoulder. "It was indeed. You were amazing. That was exactly what I'd hoped we could do. It's even better with the orange infusion your aunt added."

"I'm glad I could do something, but what exactly did the oranges do for the spell?"

"Flavor."

"What?" I asked.

Gwinn laughed. "We needed to fix the one problem with most potions. The taste. In the middle of it all, I realized that if we added something flavorful while the wild magic flowed, it would infuse the orange into the end product."

She used a spoon and sipped some of the potion. A broad grin crossed her face. "Oh my goodness. That's delightful. Try some."

Once more, she dipped the spoon into the potion. Sadie and I both took turns tasting it.

"Wow, that's delicious," Sadie said. "We did that?"

"No," Gwinn said. "You did that. That is all wild magic's work. Now we won't have to hold your friends down to get them to drink it. I was worried about that."

"That is amazing," I said. "If we bottled that, we'd make a fortune."

"Only if we want to link everyone who drinks more than a sip to Sadie forever."

I did a double take at Gwinn. "What are you talking about? Everyone who drinks from that potion is going to be tied to Sadie for eternity?"

"How else could we bring them under her royal protection? That kind of link has forever been a two-way bond. The effect will fade with time, but they'll always have a sort of fondness toward the queen. What's wrong with that?"

"I don't want my friends on the team liking me only because of some potion," Sadie said. "That's creepy."

"It's not a love potion," Gwinn explained. "It's more like a bonding of mutual aid. If you need help or are in danger, they'll know it. You'll feel the same toward them. Should one of them need help you can provide, you'll know it."

Sadie bit her lip. "I just don't want them looking at me differently. What if someone gets hurt because of me?"

"Do we have a choice?" I asked.

Gwinn shook her head. "Not really. This is the only way I know to protect them from what's coming tonight."

Sadie pointed at the orange cooler at the far end of the counter. "So we just pour that in there and take it to the game? I don't think there's enough to give everyone some unless we're very careful."

Gwinn pulled open a few drawers until she found a large strainer mesh. "Hold this. We'll pour the pot in through that to catch all the herbs and other solid stuff from the spell. Then we'll add ice and water until it's full. That should be enough for everyone to have a cupful before the game. Tell everyone it's an awesome new sports drink or something."

I held the cooler still while Sadie steadied the strainer over the top. Gwinn lifted the heavy pot up and tilted it over the mesh until all the potion was deposited inside. She set the pot down on the stove and took the strainer with the cooked herbs and dumped it all into the trash can.

Sadie's stomach growled. She laughed and clapped a hand across her belly. "I'm starving."

"Of course you are," I said. "You need to replenish your stores before the game. Go sit down and rest. I'll whip up something from the fridge for you. We can't have you passing out halfway through the match tonight."

Gwinn said, "I'll have some, too, if you don't mind. I'm a little peckish myself."

I started pulling together the makings of a pair of subs with lots of meat and cheese. While I worked, I focused on the coming night's contest. We were as ready as we could be. We even had a Valkyrie on our side. Still, everything came down to Sadie and her team now. I only hope we'd done enough. I didn't like standing on the sidelines at all.

26

Chip

"Get loaded up. We're running late," I called up the stairs to Addy and Sadie. Today, of all days, wasn't the time to drag our feet.

"Chip," Rose said as she checked her watch. "We need to go. We can't let Gorrath get the drop on us by getting set up early."

"I'm trying. You take Ingrid with you and go over now. I promise I'll be right behind you with the kids."

Rose checked her watch and cursed. "Dammit. Fine. Come on, Ingrid. Let's go!"

The Valkyrie followed Rose out the front door to head over to the high school.

Gripping the banister, I headed upstairs to see what was taking so long. Addy met me halfway up the steps. He wore one of his sister's school sweatshirts with the team mascot emblazoned on the front and carried a short battle axe in his right hand and a leather-bound book in the other.

"What are you doing?" I didn't know whether to question the axe or the book first. I didn't want him in the fight or sitting off to the side reading. We didn't know what we'd run into at the school.

"I want to be ready to fight, Uncle Chip. This is my favorite axe."

He raised the axe and then tapped the leather book cover with the axe head. "This is my demon codex tome. Aunt Rose gave it to me a few years ago. It'll help me identify what we're fighting and give us their weaknesses and the best ways to kill them."

"You can't carry the axe into the stadium at the school. There'll be security guards around. They'll stop you and make you put it back in the car, if you're lucky. Otherwise, they might just confiscate it."

Addy's shoulders sagged. "Aw, Uncle Chip. What am I supposed to do if I can't help cover Sadie's back? That's my job, you know."

"I know, but she's not queen yet, and that means you're not officially her protector. That's for me to do for now." I held out my hand for the axe. "You can bring the book if you want. No one needs to know the topic or title. Maybe it'll come in handy." I hoped not. If we got to where Addy had to identify demons from the entries in his tome, we would have a lot more to worry about.

"Get in the SUV. I'll fetch your sister."

Addy bounced past me, and I took two more steps up before Sadie appeared at the top of the stairs.

"Sorry, Uncle Chip. I beefed up my shin guards." She leaned down and rolled down one knee-high sock to reveal metal armored greaves instead of her usual plastic shin protectors.

"I have a feeling those aren't allowed."

"Neither is possessing an entire team with demons. I want to be ready for as much as I can."

I shrugged. Extra protection would come in handy tonight. "Go get in the truck. Addy's already down there. We have to go."

Sadie trotted down the stairs, and I followed her while I went through a mental checklist of everything we'd need. The orange cooler was filled with ice and water, along with the potion base they'd created. It was in the back of the SUV and ready to go. I patted the hilt of my Guardian sword to double check its location on my belt.

We went out to the garage. Everything was as prepared as I could make it. The rest depended on the players on the field. Of course, Sadie had to be there to ensure success.

The trip across town to the high school didn't take long. I don't know what I expected when I arrived, but it wasn't the sedate, slow-moving crowds I saw filing into the stadium. There was none of the shouting or cheering I expected from a big match like this one.

As I entered the lot, Patty's SUV pulled up next to mine, and she put her window down. "Chip, there's something weird going on in there. I don't think you should take the kids to the game."

"What do you mean?"

"It's like there's a spell over the whole stadium. I could sense the energy as soon as I arrived. I'm taking Astrid and a few of the other cheerleaders home. You should do the same."

"Thanks for the advice, Patty. I'll take it under advisement." I needed to get in there and see what was going on. Had Gorrath already put his plan into motion?

"Suit yourself, Chip. Don't say I didn't warn you." Patty hit the accelerator, and her SUV shot out of the parking lot and away from the trouble brewing there.

I ignored the worry building up inside and pulled into a spot beside Rose's Firebird at the edge of the lot. If we had to leave in a hurry, this would offer us the best chance at a quick getaway.

Sadie hopped out with her soccer backpack hoisted on one shoulder. She hung back with Addy and me while we carried the cooler between us. Five gallons of mostly water was heavier than you expected, especially when it had to be carried all the way to the home team's bench at the center of the sideline.

We were halfway across the strangely quiet parking lot, and none of the surrounding people said a word. They stared ahead with no acknowledgment of me or others around them. Each walked directly to the stadium's entrance gate, forming a nearly perfect straight line.

A chill spread across my chest. The charm resting there once again signaled nefarious magic in use.

"Kids, make sure your Fae charms are touching your skin. Something is going on here, and I want you both protected."

Both reached up and adjusted the charms on the silver chains hanging around their necks. The magical amulets of protection were already in place, but it didn't hurt to double check.

"What's going on, Uncle Chip?"

"I don't know. Let's find your Aunt Rose. She got here ahead of us." I twisted around, searching for my sister-in-law among the people approaching the gate.

Someone almost bumped into me as they passed, and I got a look at their strange eyes. The fully dilated pupils made their eyes appear completely black. They were all under some sort of spell.

"Chip," Rose called out from beside the gate. She waved to get my attention.

I steered the kids over to their aunt through the thickening crowd.

"Rose, what's going on with all the people?"

"It's Gorrath. This close to the rift, he's siphoning from its power and using it to enspell the entire crowd. We need to get Sadie to her team fast. They look as dazed as the crowd."

Both teams sat ramrod straight on their respective benches, facing off against each other from opposite sides of the playing field. The coach was nowhere to be seen.

"Keep Addy with you, Rose. I'll take the cooler and Sadie from here." I looked around. "Where's Ingrid?"

Rose shook her head. "As soon as we got close, she made a comment about demon spawn. Her wings sprouted from her shoulders, and she launched up into the sky. I haven't seen her since."

I searched the sky for a second but didn't see the flying Eldara.

"Chip, we have to be careful. If he's sensed Ingrid is here, Gorrath will be on the lookout for us, too. Our charms should protect us for now. Addy and I will search for Azith and Dezik. They were supposed to protect the portal and keep this kind of thing from happening."

I took the other cooler handle from Addy, letting out a puff of breath as I took the weight of the drink mixture. "Lead the way to your team, Sadie. We need to snap them out of this spell."

With her face set in grim determination, Sadie took me through the gate and onto the track surrounding the playing field.

When we got about fifteen feet from the bench, the nearest players on Sadie's team shook their heads as the future queen's sphere of protection pushed away the spell's effects.

"We have to get them to drink the potion. Wake them all up and bring them over to this end of the bench."

Another orange cooler matching mine already sat there. A plastic sleeve of cups lay on the bench beside it. I set my cooler down on a clear spot and lowered the other one to the ground.

"Come on over. I have some sports drink in the cooler to wake you all up." Sadie corralled her teammates into a cluster around me.

I held up the sleeve of cups. "Everyone, take one and drink some juice from this cooler. It'll help with the hazy feeling you have."

One at a time, the girls approached and filled their cups with the fragrant liquid. As soon as each of them took a sip, a broad grin crossed their face. Sadie's protective magic coursed through them.

"Everyone drink up," Sadie said. "It's going to be a long game, so drink all your juice."

She walked among her friends, encouraging them to finish their cups. When she got to me, she nodded at the stands full of silent and still fans. "What about them? We should've made more potion."

"I don't know that we could have. That's a lot of people out there. Look, the opposing team's bleachers are full of spellbound spectators, too."

"What do we do? It's really creepy."

"Keep your team focused and win this game. That's all you can do. I'll be right here. Your coach isn't here, so I guess it's on me to lead you all through this."

"Captains," a booming voice called from the center of the field. A trio of referees stood at the center of the pitch. Each had glowing red eyes.

"Sadie, you and Jenny go be team captains." I named the closest girl I recognized to join my niece. I followed behind them, ready to jump to their defense if needed.

Two members of the opposing team approached, their eyes glowing red as well. Apparently, the demon-possessed soccer ball had taken over the players and referees more directly than the fans.

The lead ref held Gorrath tucked under one arm. He waited until all had assembled before he began. When he spoke, it was the demon lord's voice that came out.

"I see you have come prepared for the contest, Guardian."

"The girls are ready to defend their home turf. Are we sticking to the usual rules of a soccer game?"

"Of course. Propriety must be observed for the portal to open completely. We will play the regulation ninety minutes for the win. If your paltry team of humans defeat my enhanced players, you'll close the portal forever. If not, your precious niece and every soul in this town will kneel, starting with you, Guardian."

"Let's get this kicked off, then."

The ref's voice returned to some semblance of normal. "Return to your benches and prepare to play ball."

Sadie and Jenny walked back to the bench with me.

"That was weird," Jenny said. "The whole time I stood there, I felt like something slimy was pushing at my brain."

"Just stay with Sadie. She's the one who can protect you all from that kind of feeling."

"If you say so. This whole thing is creepy. What's with the glowing eyes?"

Sadie laughed. "Glowing eyes are cool. See?" She released some of her magic, and her eyes flashed deep blue.

To my surprise, when Sadie's eyes flashed, so did Jenny's. "Hey, I think your power manifests in them, too."

Sadie laughed. "Then let's get them all glowing. We've got a match to win." Her eyes flared brighter. Around me, the entire team gasped and then started laughing with Sadie. All their eyes glowed sapphire blue to match Sadie's. The team was ready to compete against the demon-enhanced opponents.

Addy showed up, a little out of breath. He carried an axe.

"Where'd you get that?"

"Aunt Rose gave it to me. She's under the grandstand fighting someone. She told me to come find you." His eyes searched the area around the home side's bleachers.

"Don't worry about Rose. She can take care of herself. You stay here and watch my back. I need to monitor the game."

The players had taken the field. I looked across the pitch at Sadie, so much power packed into a teenager's body. All our plans, the spells, the secrets—we'd laid it all out for this moment. There was no backup plan. We were in it now.

The ref blew his whistle to start the contest. He'd given the ball to the demon team first with no coin toss. They charged down the field with the ball, making crisp, targeted passes to get past the defenders.

Initially, the home team rocked back on their heels, trying to cover the assault on their goal. Their players couldn't get to the ball.

The demons pressed hard and played rough, bowling over and through the defenders.

Sadie ran in hard, catching up to the demon-girl with the ball. With a bellowed war cry, she slid from behind, kicking the ball out from under the other girl. The opponent toppled over and tumbled across the grass.

Both players jumped to their feet, racing after the loose ball and jostling for position. It was hard to watch the rough play. The ref was doing nothing to stop it. Elbows flew, digging into ribs, each pushing the other away from the ball.

Sadie made it first, just ahead of the other player. She planted her foot and kicked the ball free in a perfect crossing pass to the player on the wing on the opposite side of the field.

The demon beside her kicked hard, not at the ball, but at Sadie's ankle.

I shouted, fearing the worst. However, the kick glanced off the armored shin guard, and the demon girl tumbled past Sadie's firmly planted leg to roll across the turf.

Sadie laughed and ran back upfield to catch up with her team's front line. They pressed the ball forward, each pass crisply moving the ball from player to player in a quick passing attack toward the demon team's goal.

One of Sadie's teammates took a shot, and the enemy goalie launched across the goal in a spectacular save right before the ball crossed the line.

"Ah, no way," I shouted. "Okay, good play. Reset now. Here they come."

Thus began a back-and-forth contest where neither team could land a goal. It was a test of endurance and will. The team that lost would be the one that ran out of magical sustenance first.

Gorrath and his proximity to the portal fueled his side. Sadie's wild

Fae magic sustained her side, each girl drawing on the power from the potion that connected them to her.

I cheered them on past the half and well into the final minutes of regulation time. Neither side had scored. But something had to tip the balance soon. If not, this would go into an overtime Gorrath couldn't lose.

27

Rose

Chip was getting our team ready for the game. That left Addy and me to track down the missing demons who were supposed to be guarding the opening between hell and the stadium. Gorrath shouldn't have been able to take hold here with them watching things.

"What do you want me to do, Aunt Rose?"

"Come with me. We need our weapons."

"Won't people notice?"

"These people are all under a spell. They won't notice anything. Even if we win, I think it'll take time for all this to wear off. When that happens, I'll call the local authorities and report a magical incursion. They can dispatch local units to clean up the mess."

Addy followed me to my car. I popped the trunk and reached inside. I found what I wanted and handed an axe to Addy. It was just about the size of his chosen weapon at home.

"Cool." He took a few practice swings with one hand and then two.

"Careful with that." I pulled out my blade from the sheath behind my seat. "If you dent one of these cars, I'll make you pay for it out of your allowance."

He stopped his wild leaps as he swung the axe around in a big loop. "Sorry. I'll be more careful."

"Come on. Azith said they'd found a spot beneath the bleachers to set up shop watching the field. We can start looking for them there."

Addy walked beside me, and we made our way back to the grandstand on the home side of the field. Going around to the rear, we found an opening in the concrete-supported bleachers. It was dark, but that was no problem for two Fae, and Addy and I both pressed forward with our innate dark sight.

The eerily silent stands above us lent a sense of doom I couldn't shake as I searched to the right and Addy looked to the left. I didn't dare ask Addy if he felt anything. I didn't want to freak him out.

"Aunt Rose, over here."

I joined Addy and nearly tripped over the bodies of Azith and Dezik. The two demons lay beside each other, still in human form. From a quick glance, I could tell they'd died fighting back-to-back. Boot prints in the dirt circled their bodies.

Azith and Dezik, dead. Their last act was to stand guard—protectors to the end. A part of me clenched. Even demons could die with honor.

I leaned forward to touch Azith's chest. Still warm. "Addy, back away." I jerked my head, searching the gloom for their attackers.

Something moved in the dark at the far side of the grandstand, and I shielded Addy with my body. "Run. Head for the field and find your uncle."

"I won't leave you. We can take them."

"No, Addy. There might be more of them. Find Chip and Sadie. Warn them."

I shoved him in the chest and sent the boy stumbling back a few steps.

He regained his balance, looked past me, and then ran back the way we'd come.

Right after Addy ran off, the lurker came close enough for me to distinguish Ingrid stalking out of the darkness. Her glowing silver blade appeared in her right hand.

I pointed at the bodies at my feet. "Did you do this? They were here watching for Gorrath."

"Careful with your tone," Ingrid cautioned. "And no, I didn't kill them. Their bodies were there when I arrived. I was seeking their attackers when I overheard you and the boy talking."

"Find anything?"

"No, but the people who did this couldn't have gone far."

Just then, eight figures materialized from the nearby darkness. Robed and hooded, the approaching cultists came armed with clubs and knives.

I faced the approaching attackers as Ingrid took up a fighting stance beside me. Sadie's battle on the field might decide the day, but she would only succeed if I stopped these goons from carrying out whatever plans they had to support Gorrath.

Knowing it was suicide to wait for them to surround us, I charged at the left side of their ragged line, my battle cry ringing out. I lunged in a feint at the figure on the end, then twisted my grip on the sword and sliced the midsection of the cultist next to him.

Ingrid raced to the right, moving faster than my eye could follow.

The nearest cultist staggered backward with a gurgling cry as my blade bit deep. I responded with a kick at the knee of my initial target, who leaped sideways to avoid my lunge. It left him flatfooted and in no position to avoid my follow-up kick to his knee.

His knee popped and crunched under my heel, and his scream resounded, high and jagged in the stillness.

He fell, clutching at his ruined leg.

Across from me, Ingrid had dispatched two more of the cultists. With four down in the initial five seconds of this battle, it was getting closer to a fair fight.

Of course, people who fought fair in a contest like this were destined to lose. I bent forward while turning to face the remaining four. With a flip of my fingers, I scooped up a handful of dirt and flung it into the eyes of the closest cultist.

He yelped and stopped his advance to clear his vision.

I charged past him, using his stumbling form to block attacks from another one. Once I went around his back, I thrust upward in a quick penetrating blow that slid between his ribs from behind, with the tip coming out from his collarbone beside his chin.

I pulled back instantly to keep my blade from getting trapped inside his collapsing body.

Seeing how quickly Ingrid and I had dispatched the initial five cultists, the rest hesitated in their advance.

Ingrid shook her head. "Classic blunder, boys. Hesitation means failure in a fight to the death."

We both lunged forward.

I tucked and rolled past the center cultist in the trio. I came up on one knee and pivoted around, leading with my blade. The longsword slashed from behind through the hamstrings of the center and right attackers.

Both tried to run, but they tumbled to the ground as their legs failed to function properly.

The final cultist dropped his spiked club and held up his hands.

It was too late. Ingrid's sword cut through his neck, severing his airway and carotid arteries on the way through.

He clutched at his ruined neck, mouth open in a silent scream with no air to support it anymore. She snapped a kick at his chest, knocking him to the ground to die.

The two with cut hamstrings crawled away, but not fast enough.

I caught the closest and dispatched him with a stab to the back. The other one I kicked in the side, rolling the hooded figure over.

The youthful, pimply-faced kid who stared up at me was a surprise. He looked little older than Sadie.

I stepped on his heaving chest to hold him still. "Where's your leader? What was your plan here underneath the bleachers?"

"We were told to wait and stop anyone who came down here."

"Who told you that?"

"G-G-Gary. The High Priest. He said he needed privacy to maintain control over the crowd on this side of the field."

Ingrid moved closer, brandishing her heavenly blade. "What's he want to do with them besides keep them silent and watching the match?"

"They're to lend their pitiful human mana to Lord Gorrath during the match to help him win. He will open the gates to hell itself."

Good. Now I knew their plan.

I raised my sword.

"No!" The kid's shout of fear made me reconsider killing him. I kicked the kid in the head to knock him out instead. Then I used my sword's weighted pommel to knock out the whimpering one whose knee I'd crushed. Every life we spared came with a risk. But damn it, I was tired of blood. I didn't want Sadie to win this game and step into a world built on corpses.

"You are too lenient," Ingrid said. "They have consorted with demons. They should pay with their lives."

"There's been too much killing here already."

"What do we do next, then?"

I flexed my fingers one at a time around the grip on my sword. "It's time to find this High Priest, Gary, and stop whatever infernal magic he's using to control the crowd on this side of the field.

"If there is someone exerting control on this side of the field, there must be someone on the opposite side, too. I will go there and root them out." Her white-feathered wings flared out behind her. She ran for the opening behind the grandstand and soared up into the night.

I refocused on finding Gary on this side of the game. A quick search of the area in the magical spectrum lit up the far corner of the bleachers near the scoreboard. It pulsed with a foul, red glow. That was Gary's location, for sure.

I trotted forward, holding my sword at the ready until I was close enough to use my Fae sight to penetrate the near-total darkness here below the grandstand. I was perhaps twenty feet away when a voice rang out from up ahead.

A dark-robed figure stepped out from behind a concrete pillar. "That's far enough, woman. You're too late to stop what happens here tonight. Soon, Lord Gorrath will usher in a new age, beginning with this small hamlet. All who live here will bow before him."

"He's a demon trapped inside a soccer ball. It's not exactly a sign of unlimited power." I took a few more steps forward, wary of a trap or other cultists nearby.

"Do not mock that which you don't understand, Fae trash. The demon lord will be free to have his way with all who stand against him. Perhaps I will even let you live long enough to fall directly before his wrath."

Gary glanced past me, searching the darkness.

"Looking for your goons, Gary? They're all dead. It only took one warrior princess to drop them all. What makes you think you'll be able to stand up to me alone?"

"I was looking for Otto, actually."

"Who's Otto?"

Gary pointed behind me. "He is."

I spun around, bringing up my sword. Overconfidence had locked my attention on Gary, and I had failed to pick up on the footsteps behind me. A giant shadow stepped forward. The minotaur swung a fist at my head before I could do more than gasp.

Pain flashed streaks of light across my vision. My knees buckled beneath me, and I lost my balance, falling forward to the dirt.

I tried to rise again, pushing back nausea and dizziness. I had to fight back against the half-bull, half-man creature.

A rock-hard hoof kicked out, striking my head.

I hit the dirt hard. The world spun. And as the shadows swallowed me, the last thing I heard was Gary's laughter.

28

Chip

The brutal game had worn out Sadie and her teammates. With no coach present, it fell to me to manage the game. I knew they needed some fresh legs, but I didn't know the team well enough to know who to sub in.

Sadie must have been thinking the same thing. During a lull in the action as the home team dribbled the ball upfield, Sadie ran past. "During the next stoppage, put in Missy, Joan, and Renata. We'll pull Sloane, Angelica, and Jenny to rest. They're gassed."

"Got it."

There were only two minutes left in regulation time. We had to score a goal now. There was no way I was going to take a chance with penalty kicks deciding this contest.

Sadie shouted at me when the ball got kicked out of bounds on the far side of the field.

I realized she wanted the subs to come in. "Missy, Joan, Renata, you're all in. Play hard, as if your lives depended on it."

The girls gave me a strange look as they jogged onto the field. They were out from under the demon's spell, but they still didn't understand the stakes of this game.

The three relieved players ran off the pitch and took seats on the bench as play resumed. The throw-in launched the ball over the heads of the nearest opponents in Sadie's direction. Her voice carried across the field as she called out a play to her teammates.

As soon as the ball reached her, she headed it away to a teammate and ran downfield. Her team's line advanced. Their crisp passes evaded the demon-possessed defenders.

I checked the scoreboard. The clock ticked down to less than a minute in the match.

Sadie crossed toward the opponent's goal right behind a perfect pass. She yelled out her war cry, and her entire form lit up, outlined in sapphire-blue light.

Her foot came forward and connected in a perfectly timed kick.

The goalie got caught leaning the wrong direction, and Sadie sent the ball into the corner of the goal, just inside the post.

A cheer went up from our bench, the only sound in the strangely silent stadium.

On the field, Sadie's teammates mobbed around her as she raced back toward midfield.

The buzzer sounded a few seconds later, announcing the end of regulation play. We'd won.

Addy and I hugged and jumped up and down, thinking that was the end of it.

A bellowing roar sounded behind us.

I spun around, my hand instinctively going to my sword's hilt at my belt.

Beside me, Addy hefted the war axe.

A giant beast, half man, half bull, charged at us from an opening beneath the stands. Behind him came a robed figure carrying a glowing red soccer ball. Gorrath was making one last play. Deep inside, I knew the demon could still win if he were brought to the portal.

"Addy, I'll take the bull thing. You get to that ball and keep them from reaching the field with it."

"It's a minotaur, Uncle Chip. Be careful, they're super strong."

On the pitch, the demon-possessed opponents screamed and rushed our way. Sadie rallied her teammates to stop them, and nearly a dozen individual fistfights broke out across the field.

The minotaur charged at me, bellowing as he lowered his horns for the final rush. I'd read mythology books, but nothing prepared me for that much muscle and rage.

I extended my blade to its full length and considered my options. The creature was nearly eight feet tall. I couldn't stand up to it in a head-on fight.

An idea came to me. I raised my Guardian barrier, but only to make it stand a foot above the ground, directly in the path of the charging creature.

The invisible force field caught the minotaur at his shins. He tripped forward and tumbled head over heels to the ground directly in front of me.

I didn't hesitate. I aimed for the back of its neck with my sword, knowing I couldn't let it stand up again. It would destroy the entire team with its power.

The man-bull had started to climb onto its hands and knees when my blade came down. I chopped into its thick neck.

The blow reverberated up the sword into my arm. It was like chopping a block of oak.

I pulled back and hacked down again.

The injured minotaur still struggled to rise. It got up on its knees and pivoted its red, glowing eyes my way.

I swung with all my force at its neck again and again until its head tumbled to the grass beside its body.

My breaths came in gasps. I stepped back and searched for Addy.

The cult leader had my nephew locked in a fight, Addy's axe versus a curved scimitar.

I had to admit, the kid had skill. He kept the cultist back from the field. It helped that the man held onto the glowing ball with one hand while he fought. Addy used that awkwardness to his advantage.

I drew upon more of my mana and formed my Guardian barrier into a six-inch-diameter globe. It launched out from my hand at high speed and caught the robed cultist in the small of his back.

The blow caught him by surprise. Gorrath flew free of his grasp as the cultist pitched forward to the ground.

I ran over and kicked him in the head three times until he'd stopped groaning and trying to rise.

"Radical, Uncle Chip," Addy said. He walked over to the ball and looked over at me. "What do we do with this?"

Ingrid swooped down from the sky and landed beside us. "Your sister knows what must be done."

"I'll take it," Sadie called out. She ran over from the center of the field to the sideline.

My Guardian senses clamored with danger signals. "Sadie, do you know what to do?"

"I think so. It's time to send this thing back to where it came from."

Sadie's body glowed again with the outline of her Fae power. She bent forward to pick up the ball and carried it over to just past midfield. This was where it had all started, over a week before.

"No! Stop!" Gorrath's voice echoed around the field from nowhere and everywhere all at once. It even broadcast over the stadium's loudspeakers.

All action on the pitch had stopped. The fighting between the teams ceased as each girl turned to watch Sadie.

The demon's voice howled desperately. "You cannot defeat me. You're nothing but a little girl."

Ingrid called out from beside me. "Tell him the truth, Sadie. This is your moment."

"Gorrath, you are wrong. I am Sadie Proctor. I am the heir to the Fae queens of old. My power holds sway in this place, not yours."

A gasp went up from the assembled crowd. Sadie's words had broken the spell over them. People called out from everywhere in the stands, questioning what had happened.

I walked over to stand beside my niece.

Twenty feet away, the ground opened up. A flaming soccer goal with a net of barbed wire rose from the rift. A tall demon with red and green scales stood in the goal, bent over in a ready position.

Sadie set Gorrath down on the grass, which smoked and sizzled from contact with the glowing demonic ball. "One more shot to make."

"You've got this, kiddo." I stepped back as Sadie took up a position a few feet behind the ball.

A loud, shrill steam whistle jutted up from one of the corner posts, its piercing sound cutting through the shouts from the stands.

It was time to take the shot.

Sadie nodded, still outlined in blue power. She charged forward and launched the ball at the left corner.

The demon goalie dove to the correct side, punching out and blocking the ball as it came in.

My heart skipped a beat. The air went still.

For a second, the whole stadium froze, as if history itself held its breath. Had we lost after everything we had worked for?

The blocked ball arched through the air.

Her position was all wrong, but somehow Sadie leaped up, leaning back as far as she could, and executed a textbook bicycle kick to send the ball into the opposite side of the goal.

The demon goalie tried to get up when it saw what she was doing, but it was too late.

Gorrath the demon soccer ball slammed back into the barbed-wire net and stuck there.

A rumbling shook the entire stadium as another earthquake rolled across the field.

I struggled to keep my feet while my eyes were glued to the hell goal. Slowly, it sank back into the ground, carrying both the goalie and the demon ball with it.

Gorrath's voice howled and railed against the forces dragging him downward. "I will return! No child can hold back the tide of hell forever!" Then, he was gone, and silence fell over the field.

And just like that, the demon lord was sent screaming back to hell —defeated by cleats, courage, and a girl who'd finally claimed her crown.

29

Rose

Something shook me. It took me a second to realize it was the ground itself, rumbling in another earthquake. I rose on one elbow and looked around. Where the hell was I?

I remembered fighting Gary, the cult leader, and then the minotaur. I was sure I had died at the end of that fight.

"Rose, where are you?" Chip called out my name.

"She's over here!" Addy shouted. He ran over and knelt down beside me. "Are you all right, Aunt Rose?"

My hand came away from my forehead, sticky with blood. "I'll be okay."

Chip, Sadie, and Ingrid appeared beside Addy, worry etched across their faces.

"Did you do it?" I asked.

Chip's broad grin lit up his face. "Sadie was wonderful. She rallied her team and won the game, then sent Gorrath on his way back to hell."

"The girl fought well, with skill and tenacity," Ingrid added.

A strange mix of pride and helplessness twisted in my gut. I'd missed the moment. My girl had stood without me. And maybe… that was okay.

"I can't wait to hear all about it." I struggled to my feet, still a little dizzy.

Chip bent down and retrieved my sword. "We should go. The local authorities have arrived and are checking around to find out more about what happened. There are a lot of bodies under here that we don't want to explain."

"Agreed. Lead the way."

I stumbled on the uneven ground, and two steady hands caught me, Addy on one side, Sadie on the other. It felt strange to rely on their help, but I realized they were growing up and would be expected to do more and more in the coming years. I leaned on them as I walked, slowly regaining my bearings and strength.

Chip led the way in a roundabout route back to the car. We avoided the police, who mostly clustered around the pitch, which had a huge burning gash near midfield. A fire truck had arrived, and the firefighters pulled a long hose from the front of the truck in the parking lot to dowse the flames dotting the field.

We reached my Firebird and Chip's SUV without being stopped by anyone. I stowed my sword back in its sheath behind my seat.

"Can you drive?" Chip asked. "We could leave the Firebird here and come back later."

"Better to take it now than to leave it for police to find and wonder about. I'll be fine."

"I'll accompany her," Ingrid offered. "She will return safely. I swear it."

I opened my mouth to protest and decided it wasn't worth it. Chip was right to worry. I was more than a little woozy.

"Hey," Sadie said, her face lit up with a smile. "If this had happened a year from now, I'd be able to drive you home."

That thought sent a fresh shiver down my spine. I definitely wasn't ready for her to drive yet. I just nodded and climbed into the Firebird, trying to hide my sore groan as I slid into the seat. Ingrid walked around to the passenger side.

Chip must've heard me groan. He leaned over. "Hey, you leave first, and I'll follow you. If you need to, pull into a store lot and park.

We'll come back and get it from there later. The police won't make a connection that way."

"I'll be fine." I nodded at Sadie, who stood nearby, watching the dazed and confused people file out of the stadium. "She did good?"

"Better than good. I got a glimpse of the warrior queen within her today. She's almost ready, I think."

"Gods, that's the scariest thing yet. Don't rush it. We have three more years before we have to cross that particular bridge."

Chip laughed. "She's headed there fast, whether or not we like it. I fear we're just along for the ride now."

"We've gotten her this far. I guess we'll have to let go eventually." I reached up and gripped Chip's hand where it rested on the door. "We're not a bad team after all."

"No, we're not. But then, I've known that about the two of us for a very long time." He gave my hand a squeeze and stepped back.

I recognized that glint in his eye from a long time ago. The strange thing was, it didn't bother me the way it usually did. Chip had changed, and so had I. Maybe it was time to consider an adjustment to the status quo. I'd have to think about it while we finished out this year.

Chip got in the SUV with Sadie and Addy.

I backed out once Ingrid had climbed in beside me. We started for home while a thousand thoughts swirled in my fuzzy brain. In the whirlwind of pain, fatigue, and relief, one image lingered: Sadie, radiant and unshakable, stepping into the light of the crown she was born to wear.

<hr>

Are you ready for the stunning series finale, *Graduation Fae*? Get your preorder in now!

Also by Jamie Davis

Get a free book and updates for new books.

visit JamieDavisBooks.com/send-free-book/

Extreme Medical Services Series

(A 9-book Urban Fantasy series starting with)

Book 1 - Extreme Medical Services

—

Eldara Sister Series

The Nightingale's Angel

Blue and Gray Angel

—

Lone Wolf Squadron Series

(a 9-book Space Western series starting with)

Marshal the Stars

—

The Huntress Clan Saga

(A 6-book Urban Fantasy series starting with)

Huntress Initiate

—

The Broken Throne Series

(A 5-Book Dystopian Urban Fantasy

starting with)

The Charm Runner

—

The Accidental Traveler LitRPG Series

(with C.J. Davis)

(A 6-book Epic Fantasy Series starting with)

The Accidental Thief

—

Follow on Facebook for updates, news, and upcoming book excerpts

Jamie's Fun Fantasy Readers Facebook Group

Help the Author

I Need Your Help ...

Without reviews indie books like this one are almost impossible to market.

Leaving a review will only take a minute — it doesn't have to be long or involved, just a sentence or two that tells people what you liked about the book, to help other readers know why they might like it, too. It also helps me write more of what you love.

The truth is, VERY few readers leave reviews. Please help me out by being the exception.

Thank you in advance!

Jamie Davis

About the Author

Jamie Davis writes stories where magic meets heart and family saves the day.

A nurse, retired paramedic, and lifelong gamer, Jamie brings a deep love of sci-fi, fantasy, and found family to every tale he tells—whether it's an enchanted road trip, a demon-possessed soccer ball, or a suburban uncle navigating fae politics with a toddler in tow. His books mix real-world emotion with wild, magical twists, and always leave room for a laugh (or a heartfelt tear).

When he's not writing or rolling dice, Jamie lives in the woods of Maryland with his wife, their three kids, and a dog who thinks she's the real hero of the story. He's the creator of Fun Fantasy Reads, a growing collection of novels across urban fantasy, LitRPG, sci-fi, and contemporary paranormal genres.

Jamie loves connecting with fans at cons and online—so don't be shy. Visit JamieDavisBooks.com for new releases, free stories, and more chances to escape into adventure.

Follow Jamie Online

facebook.com/jamiedavisbooks

instagram.com/podmedic